SIR GAWAIN AND THE GREEN KNIGHT

Translated by Jessie Weston

COLLINS
CLASSICS

William Collins
An imprint of HarperCollins*Publishers*
1 London Bridge Street
London SE1 9GF

WilliamCollinsBooks.com

HarperCollins*Publishers*
1st Floor, Watermarque Building, Ringsend Road
Dublin 4, Ireland

This William Collins paperback edition published in Great Britain in 2021

1

A catalogue record for this book
is available from the British Library

ISBN 978-0-00-848553-5; 978-0-00-848555-9

Life & Times section © HarperCollins*Publishers* Ltd
Fran Fabriczki asserts her moral right as the author of the Life & Times section
Classic Literature: Words and Phrases adapted from
Collins English Dictionary

All rights reserved. No part of this publication may be
reproduced, stored in a retrieval system, or transmitted,
in any form or by any means, electronic, mechanical,
photocopying, recording or otherwise, without the
prior permission of the publishers.

This book is sold subject to the condition that it shall not,
by way of trade or otherwise, be lent, re-sold, hired out or otherwise
circulated without the publisher's prior consent in any form of
binding or cover other than that in which it is published and
without a similar condition including this condition being
imposed on the subsequent purchaser.

Typesetting in Kalix by Palimpsest Book Production Limited,
Falkirk, Stirlingshire

Printed and bound in Great Britain by CPI Group (UK) Ltd,
Croydon CR0 4YY

MIX
Paper from
responsible sources
FSC™ C007454

This book is produced from independently certified FSC™ paper
to ensure responsible forest management.

For more information visit: www.harpercollins.co.uk/green

History of William Collins

In 1819, millworker William Collins from Glasgow, Scotland, set up a company for printing and publishing pamphlets, sermons, hymn books, and prayer books. That company was Collins and was to mark the birth of HarperCollins Publishers as we know it today. The long tradition of Collins dictionary publishing can be traced back to the first dictionary William co-published in 1825, *Greek and English Lexicon*. Indeed, from 1840 onwards, he began to produce illustrated dictionaries and even obtained a licence to print and publish the Bible.

Soon after, William published the first Collins novel; however, it was the time of the Long Depression, where harvests were poor, prices were high, potato crops had failed, and violence was erupting in Europe. As a result, many factories across the country were forced to close down and William chose to retire in 1846, partly due to the hardships he was facing.

Aged 30, William's son, William II, took over the business. A keen humanitarian with a warm heart and a generous spirit, William II was truly "Victorian" in his outlook. He introduced new, up-to-date steam presses and published affordable editions of Shakespeare's works and *The Pilgrim's Progress*, making them available to the masses for the first time.

A new demand for educational books meant that success came with the publication of travel books, scientific books, encyclopedias, and dictionaries. This demand to be educated led to the later publication of atlases, and Collins also held the monopoly on scripture writing at the time.

TRANSLATED BY JESSIE WESTON

In the 1860s Collins began to expand and diversify and the idea of "books for the millions" was developed, although the phrase wasn't coined until 1907. Affordable editions of classical literature were published, and in 1903 Collins introduced 10 titles in their Collins Handy Illustrated Pocket Novels. These proved so popular that a few years later this had increased to an output of 50 volumes, selling nearly half a million in their year of publication. In the same year, The Everyman's Library was also instituted, with the idea of publishing an affordable library of the most important classical works, biographies, religious and philosophical treatments, plays, poems, travel, and adventure. This series eclipsed all competition at the time, and the introduction of paperback books in the 1950s helped to open that market and marked a high point in the industry.

HarperCollins is and has always been a champion of the classics, and the current Collins Classics series follows in this tradition—publishing classical literature that is affordable and available to all. Beautifully packaged, highly collectible, and intended to be reread and enjoyed at every opportunity.

Life and Times

Not many readers would immediately recognize the English language in the original text of the poem 'Sir Gawain and the Green Knight' – and yet, the work is a contemporary of Chaucer's *The Canterbury Tales*, and both are seminal works of Middle English literature. After being lost for centuries, almost being burnt in a fire and languishing in the British Library, 'Sir Gawain and the Green Knight' has finally taken its place amongst the great texts of medieval English poetry.

The poet

While it's difficult to state many biographical facts about the poet behind 'Sir Gawain and the Green Knight' with confidence, academics have made attempts to reconstruct some of their background. An important clue in understanding who the 'Gawain-poet' was lies in the manuscript itself, which also contained three other poems – 'Pearl', 'Patience', and 'Purity'. Although we can't know for sure that all of these works were written by the same author, textual analysis indicates that they were. From these texts – both the dialect used, and the topographical references – academics have deduced that the poet must have been from the Cheshire area. It can also be inferred from the Christian subject-matter of three of the poems that the poet was religious, although 'Gawain', an Arthurian romance, is somewhat of an outlier in that respect. However, the overtly Christian subject-matter of the other poems in the manuscript has led some academics to interpret 'Gawain' through the lens of Christianity as well, commenting on the frequent Biblical references, and the complexities of Gawain's moral dilemma that goes beyond a simple adherence to the 'chivalric code' of the time.

Style

The poem was originally written in alliterative verse, which was the form commonly used in Old English poetry, but was also popular among the fourteenth and fifteenth century Middle English poets. Unlike the metrical forms we are accustomed to in English poetry today, which rely on syllabic count and rhyme schemes, alliterative verse usually contained a pair of stressed syllables and a caesura. It is likely that the poem was enjoyed aurally, and the musicality of the original comes to life most when recited.

The first modern translation of the text by Jessie Weston in 1898 interprets the Middle English poem into modern prose for a retelling that preserves both the spirit of the original and makes it accessible to modern readers.

The chivalric code

The beliefs that guide Gawain's actions and propels the narrative is the so-called 'chivalric code'. This wasn't a fixed, static code, but rather something that developed over time, initially as a way to regulate the behaviour of knights at a time of constant war, especially during the Crusades in the eleventh and twelfth centuries. Initially the qualities espoused were to do with discipline in battle – a knight must be brave on the battlefield and loyal to his lord. But later, this set of values was expanded through to the romances written at the time – knights represented as devoutly Christian, courteous and caring for the well-being of others. There was likely a large discrepancy between the actual behaviour of crusading armies and their fictional counterparts, but in the Arthurian legends, at least, knights were often measured against their ability to keep to this chivalric code.

In the poem, Gawain is presented as a paragon of chivalry from the beginning – he intervenes on Arthur's behalf, taking on the challenge of the Green Knight in place of his lord. Later on, when he is a guest at Bertilak's castle, at the centre of his dilemma is the fact that as part of the chivalric code he must honour his host, and show loyalty to his lord, but he must also be courteous to the lady. Gawain manages to maintain the balance until –swayed by the prospect of his own death – he both accepts a gift from the lady, lies to his lord, and flinches at the axe, thus revealing a lack of bravery. And yet, neither the lord nor his fellow knights of the Round Table begrudge him these faults, and readers are left to wonder to what extent the chivalric code can truly govern a knight's actions. Knowing when to deviate from it ends up saving Gawain's life.

Arthurian romance tradition

The legend of a warrior and king named Arthur was pieced together throughout the middle ages: in the twelfth century, Geoffrey of Monmouth, in his *History of the Kings of Britain*, solidified the legend, while elements of it were taken up by French writers such as Chrétien de Troyes and Marie de France, who further developed the legend of Arthur, including prominent elements such as the Round Table.

These were popular texts at the time when this poet likely composed 'Sir Gawain and the Green Knight' and the text shows a familiarity with these works, as well as an understanding that the readers would be familiar with its allusions and contexts. It contains many of the elements of a traditional

TRANSLATED BY JESSIE WESTON

Arthurian romance: a threat from outside the Round Table, a young knight ready to prove himself and a quest worthy of his abilities. As Gawain travels to Bertilak's castle, he encounters many of the traditional tests of merit that chivalric heroes must undergo – harsh weather conditions, mythical beasts to slay – and yet the poet moves swiftly past these, as though Gawain's quest were more than a simple hero's journey, and at Bertilak's castle, his tests become more internalised, and value-based.

The poem opens and ends with a reference to Troy, effectively tying this Arthurian legend to the Ancient Greek epic tradition, through the legend of Brutus's founding of Britain. The complex moral dilemma at the heart of the story, along with frequent references to Christianity and its framing through the lens of antiquity, gives a sense of striving towards something beyond a simple variation on the Arthurian legend.

Sir Gawain and the Green Knight

CONTENTS

Sir Gawain and the Green Knight, in prose 1
Sir Gawain and the Green Knight, in poetry 55

Classic Literature: Words and Phrases 161

BOOK I

OF THE MAKING OF BRITAIN
After the siege and the assault of Troy, when that burg was destroyed and burnt to ashes, and the traitor tried for his treason, the noble Æneas and his kin sailed forth to become princes and patrons of well-nigh all the Western Isles. Thus Romulus built Rome (and gave to the city his own name, which it bears even to this day); and Ticius turned him to Tuscany; and Langobard raised him up dwellings in Lombardy; and Felix Brutus sailed far over the French flood, and founded the kingdom of Britain, wherein have been war and waste and wonder, and bliss and bale, ofttimes since.

And in that kingdom of Britain have been wrought more gallant deeds than in any other; but of all British kings Arthur was the most valiant, as I have heard tell; therefore will I set forth a wondrous adventure that fell out in his time. And if ye will listen to me, but for a little while, I will tell it even as it stands in my story stiff and strong, fixed in the letter, as it hath long been known in the land.

HOW ARTHUR HELD HIGH FEAST AT CAMELOT
King Arthur lay at Camelot upon a Christmas-tide, with many a gallant lord and lovely lady, and all the noble brotherhood

of the Round Table. There they held rich revels with gay talk and jest; one while they would ride forth to joust and tourney, and again back to the court to make carols; for there was the feast holden fifteen days with all the mirth that men could devise, song and glee, glorious to hear, in the daytime, and dancing at night. Halls and chambers were crowded with noble guests, the bravest of knights and the loveliest of ladies, and Arthur himself was the comeliest king that ever held a court. For all this fair folk were in their youth, the fairest and most fortunate under heaven, and the king himself of such fame that it were hard now to name so valiant a hero.

NEW YEAR'S DAY

Now the New Year had but newly come in, and on that day a double portion was served on the high table to all the noble guests, and thither came the king with all his knights, when the service in the chapel had been sung to an end. And they greeted each other for the New Year, and gave rich gifts, the one to the other (and they that received them were not wroth, that may ye well believe!), and the maidens laughed and made mirth till it was time to get them to meat. Then they washed and sat them down to the feast in fitting rank and order, and Guinevere the queen, gaily clad, sat on the high daïs. Silken was her seat, with a fair canopy over her head, of rich tapestries of Tars, embroidered, and studded with costly gems; fair she was to look upon, with her shining grey eyes, a fairer woman might no man boast himself of having seen.

But Arthur would not eat till all were served, so full of joy and gladness was he, even as a child; he liked not either to lie long, or to sit long at meat, so worked upon him his young blood and his wild brain. And another custom he had also, that came of his nobility, that he would never eat upon an high day till he had been advised of some knightly deed, or some strange and marvelous tale, of his ancestors, or of arms, or of other ventures. Or till some stranger knight should seek of him leave to joust with one of the Round Table, that they might set their lives in jeopardy, one against another, as fortune might favour them. Such was the king's custom when he sat in hall at each high feast with his noble knights, therefore on that New year tide, he abode, fair of face, on the throne, and made much mirth withal.

OF THE NOBLE KNIGHTS THERE PRESENT

Thus the king sat before the high tables, and spake of many things; and there good Sir Gawain was seated by Guinevere the queen, and on her other side sat Agravain, *à la dure main*; both were the king's sister's sons and full gallant knights. And at the end of the table was Bishop Bawdewyn, and Ywain, King Urien's son, sat at the other side alone. These were worthily served on the daïs, and at the lower tables sat many valiant knights. Then they bare the first course with the blast of trumpets and waving of banners, with the sound of drums and pipes, of song and lute, that many a heart was uplifted at the melody. Many were the dainties, and rare the meats, so great was the plenty they might scarce find room on the board to set on the dishes. Each helped himself as he liked best, and to each two were twelve dishes, with great plenty of beer and wine.

THE COMING OF THE GREEN KNIGHT

Now I will say no more of the service, but that ye may know there was no lack, for there drew near a venture that the folk might well have left their labor to gaze upon. As the sound of the music ceased, and the first course had been fitly served, there came in at the hall door one terrible to behold, of stature greater than any on earth; from neck to loin so strong and thickly made, and with limbs so long and so great that he seemed even as a giant. And yet he was but a man, only the mightiest that might mount a steed; broad of chest and shoulders and slender of waist, and all his features of like fashion; but men marveled much at his color, for he rode even as a knight, yet was green all over.

TRANSLATED BY JESSIE WESTON

THE FASHION OF THE KNIGHT

For he was clad all in green, with a straight coat, and a mantle above; all decked and lined with fur was the cloth and the hood that was thrown back from his locks and lay on his shoulders. Hose had he of the same green, and spurs of bright gold with silken fastenings richly worked; and all his vesture was verily green. Around his waist and his saddle were bands with fair stones set upon silken work, 'twere too long to tell of all the trifles that were embroidered thereon – birds and insects in gay gauds of green and gold.

OF THE KNIGHT'S STEED

All the trappings of his steed were of metal of like enamel, even the stirrups that he stood in stained of the same, and stirrups and saddle-bow alike gleamed and shone with green stones. Even the steed on which he rode was of the same hue, a green horse, great and strong, and hard to hold, with broidered bridle, meet for the rider.

The knight was thus gaily dressed in green, his hair falling around his shoulders, on his breast hung a beard, as thick and green as a bush, and the beard and the hair of his head were clipped all round above his elbows. The lower part of his sleeves was fastened with clasps in the same wise as a king's mantle. The horse's mane was crisp and plaited with many a knot folded in with gold thread about the fair green, here a twist of the hair, here another of gold. The tail was twined in like manner, and both were bound about with a band of bright green set with many a precious stone; then they were tied aloft in a cunning knot, whereon rang many bells of burnished gold. Such a steed might no other ride, nor had such ever been looked upon in that hall ere that time; and all who saw that knight spake and said that a man might scarce abide his stroke.

SIR GAWAIN AND THE GREEN KNIGHT

THE ARMING OF THE KNIGHT

The knight bore no helm nor hauberk, neither gorget nor breast-plate, neither shaft nor buckler to smite nor to shield, but in one hand he had a holly-bough, that is greenest when the groves are bare, and in his other an axe, huge and uncomely, a cruel weapon in fashion, if one would picture it. The head was an ell-yard long, the metal all of green steel and gold, the blade burnished bright, with a broad edge, as well shapen to shear as a sharp razor. The steel was set into a strong staff, all bound round with iron, even to the end, and engraved with green in cunning work. A lace was twined about it, that looped at the head, and all adown the handle it was clasped with tassels on buttons of bright green richly broidered.

The knight rideth through the entrance of the hall, driving straight to the high daïs, and greeted no man, but looked ever upwards; and the first words he spake were, 'Where is the ruler of this folk? I would gladly look upon that hero, and have speech with him.' He cast his eyes on the knights, and mustered them up and down, striving ever to see who of them was of most renown.

Then was there great gazing to behold that chief, for each man marveled what it might mean that a knight and his steed should have even such a hue as the green grass; and that seemed even greener than green enamel on bright gold. All looked on him as he stood, and drew near unto him wondering greatly what he might be; for many marvels had they seen, but none such as this, and phantasm and faërie did the folk deem it. Therefore were the gallant knights slow to answer, and gazed astounded, and sat stone still in a deep silence through that goodly hall, as if a slumber were fallen upon them. I deem it was not all for doubt, but some for courtesy that they might give ear unto his errand.

Then Arthur beheld this adventurer before his high daïs, and knightly he greeted him, for fearful was he never. 'Sir,' he said, 'thou art welcome to this place – lord of this hall am

I, and men call me Arthur. Light thee down, and tarry awhile, and what thy will is, that shall we learn after.'

OF THE KNIGHT'S CHALLENGE

'Nay,' quoth the stranger, 'so help me He that sitteth on high, 'twas not mine errand to tarry any while in this dwelling; but the praise of this thy folk and thy city is lifted up on high, and thy warriors are holden for the best and the most valiant of those who ride mail-clad to the fight. The wisest and the worthiest of this world are they, and well proven in all knightly sports. And here, as I have heard tell, is fairest courtesy, therefore have I come hither as at this time. Ye may be sure by the branch that I bear here that I come in peace, seeking no strife. For had I willed to journey in warlike guise I have at home both hauberk and helm, shield and shining spear, and other weapons. to mine hand, but since I seek no war, my raiment is that of peace. But if thou be as bold as all men tell, thou wilt freely grant me the boon I ask.'

And Arthur answered, 'Sir Knight, if thou cravest battle here thou shalt not fail for lack of a foe.'

And the knight answered, 'Nay, I ask no fight, in faith here on the benches are but beardless children; were I clad in armour on my steed there is no man here might match me. Therefore I ask in this court but a Christmas jest, for that it is Yule-tide, and New Year, and there are here many fain for sport. If any one in this hall holds himself so hardy, so bold both of blood and brain, as to dare strike me one stroke for another, I will give him as a gift this axe, which is heavy enough, in sooth, to handle as he may list, and I will abide the first blow, unarmed as I sit. If any knight be so bold as to prove my words, let him come swiftly to me here, and take this weapon, I quit claim to it, he may keep it as is own, and I will abide his stroke, firm on the floor. Then shalt thou give me the right to deal him another, the respite of a year and a day shall he have. Now haste, and let see whether any here dare say aught.'

SIR GAWAIN AND THE GREEN KNIGHT

THE SILENCE OF THE KNIGHTS

Now if the knights had been astounded at the first, yet stiller were they all, high and low, when they had heard his words. The knight on his steed straightened himself in the saddle, and rolled his eyes fiercely round the hall, red they gleamed under his green and bushy brows. He frowned and twisted his beard, waiting to see who should rise, and when none answered he cried aloud in mockery, 'What, is this Arthur's hall, and these the knights whose renown hath run through many realms? Where are now your pride and your conquests, your wrath, and anger, and mighty words? Now are the praise and the renown of the Round Table overthrown by one man's speech, since all keep silence for dread ere ever they have seen a blow!'

With that he laughed so loudly that the blood rushed to the king's fair face for very shame; he waxed wroth, as did all his knights, and sprang to his feet, and drew near to the stranger and said, 'Now by heaven, foolish is thy asking, and thy folly shall find its fitting answer. I know no man aghast at thy great words. Give me here thine axe and I shall grant thee the boon thou hast asked.' Lightly he sprang to him and caught at his hand, and the knight, fierce of aspect, lighted down from his charger.

Then Arthur took the axe and gripped the haft, and swung it round, ready to strike. And the knight stood before him, taller by the head than any in the hall; he stood, and stroked his beard, and drew down his coat, no more dismayed for the king's threats than if one had brought him a drink of wine.

HOW SIR GAWAIN DARED THE VENTURE

Then Gawain, who sat by the queen, leaned forward to the king and spake, 'I beseech ye, my lord, let this venture be mine. Would ye but bid me rise from this seat, and stand by your side, so that my liege lady thought it not ill, then would I come to your counsel before this goodly court. For I think it not seemly when such challenges be made in your hall that ye yourself should undertake it, while there are many bold knights who sit beside ye, none are there, methinks, of readier will under heaven, or more valiant in open field. I am the weakest, I wot, and the feeblest of wit, and it will be the less loss of my life if ye seek sooth. For save that ye are mine uncle, naught is there in me to praise, no virtue is there in my body save your blood, and since this challenge is such folly that it beseems ye not to take it, and I have asked it from ye first, let it fall to me, and if I bear myself ungallantly, then let all this court blame me.'

Then they all spake with one voice that the king should leave this venture and grant it to Gawain.

Then Arthur commanded the knight to rise, and he rose up quickly and knelt down before the king, and caught hold of the weapon; and the king loosed his hold of it, and lifted up his hand, and gave him his blessing, and bade him be strong both of heart and hand. 'Keep thee well, nephew,' quoth Arthur, 'that thou give him but the one blow, and if thou redest him rightly I trow thou shalt well abide the stroke he may give thee after.'

THE MAKING OF THE COVENANT

Gawain stepped to the stranger, axe in hand, and he, never fearing, awaited his coming. Then the Green Knight spake to Sir Gawain, 'Make we our covenant ere we go further. First, I ask thee, knight, what is thy name? Tell me truly, that I may know thee.'

'In faith,' quoth the good knight, 'Gawain am I, who give thee this buffet, let what may come of it; and at this time twelvemonth will I take another at thine hand with whatsoever weapon thou wilt, and none other.'

Then the other answered again, 'Sir Gawain, so may I thrive as I am fain to take this buffet at thine hand,' and he quoth further, 'Sir Gawain, it liketh me well that I shall take at thy fist that which I have asked here, and thou hast readily and truly rehearsed all the covenant that I asked of the king, save that thou shalt swear me, by thy troth, to seek me thyself wherever thou hopest that I may be found, and win thee such reward as thou dealest me to-day, before this folk.'

'Where shall I seek thee?' quoth Gawain. 'Where is thy place? By him that made me, I wot never where thou dwellest, nor know I thee, knight, thy court, nor thy name. But teach me truly all that pertaineth thereto, and tell me thy name, and I shall use all my wit to win my way thither, and that I swear thee for sooth, and by my sure troth.'

'That is enough in the New Year, it needs no more,' quoth the Green Knight to the gallant Gawain, 'if I tell thee truly when I have taken the blow, and thou hast smitten me; then will I teach thee of my house and home, and mine own name, then mayest thou ask thy road and keep covenant. And if I waste no words then farest thou the better, for thou canst dwell in thy land, and seek no further. But take now thy toll, and let see how thou strikest.'

'Gladly will I,' quoth Gawain, handling his axe.

THE GIVING OF THE BLOW
Then the Green Knight swiftly made him ready, he bowed down his head, and laid his long locks on the crown that his bare neck might be seen. Gawain gripped his axe and raised it on high, the left foot he set forward on the floor, and let the blow fall lightly on the bare neck. The sharp edge of the blade sundered the bones, smote through the neck, and clave it in two, so that the edge of the steel bit on the ground, and the fair head fell to the earth that many struck it with their feet as it rolled forth.

THE MARVEL OF THE GREEN KNIGHT
The blood spurted forth, and glistened on the green raiment, but the knight neither faltered nor fell; he started forward with out-stretched hand, and caught the head, and lifted it up; then he turned to his steed, and took hold of the bridle, set his foot in the stirrup, and mounted. His head he held by the hair, in his hand. Then he seated himself in his saddle as if naught

ailed him, and he were not headless. He turned his steed about, the grim corpse bleeding freely the while, and they who looked upon him doubted them much for the covenant.

For he held up the head in his hand, and turned the face towards them that sat on the high daïs, and it lifted up the eyelids and looked upon them and spake as ye shall hear. 'Look, Gawain, that thou art ready to go as thou hast promised, and seek leally till thou find me, even as thou hast sworn in this hall in the hearing of these knights. Come thou, I charge thee, to the Green Chapel; such a stroke as thou hast dealt thou hast deserved, and it shall be promptly paid thee on New Year's morn. Many men know me as the knight of the Green Chapel, and if thou askest, thou shalt not fail to find me. Therefore it behooves thee to come, or to yield thee as recreant.'

With that he turned his bridle, and galloped out at the hall door, his head in his hands, so that the sparks flew from beneath his horse's hoofs. Whither he went none knew, no more than they wist whence he had come; and the king and Gawain they gazed and laughed, for in sooth this had proved a greater marvel than any they had known aforetime.

Though Arthur the king was astonished at his heart, yet he let no sign of it be seen, but spake in courteous wise to the fair queen: 'Dear lady, be not dismayed, such craft is well suited to Christmas-tide when we seek jesting, laughter, and song, and fair carols of knights and ladies. But now I may well get me to meat, for I have seen a marvel I may not forget.' Then he looked on Sir Gawain, and said gaily, 'Now, fair nephew, hang up thine axe, since it has hewn enough,' and they hung it on the dossal above the dais, where all men might look on it for a marvel, and by its true token tell of the wonder. Then the twain sat them down together, the king and the good knight, and men served them with a double portion, as was the share of the noblest, with all manner of meat and of minstrelsy. And they spent that day in gladness, but Sir Gawain must well bethink him of the heavy venture to which he had set his hand.

BOOK II

This beginning of adventures had Arthur at the New Year, for he yearned to hear gallant tales, though his words were few when he sat at the feast. But now had they stern work on hand. Gawain was glad to begin the jest in the hall, but ye need have no marvel if the end be heavy. For though a man be merry in mind when he has well drunk, yet a year runs full swiftly, and the beginning but rarely matches the end.

THE WANING OF THE YEAR
For Yule was now over-past, and the year after, each season in its turn following the other. For after Christmas comes crabbed Lent, that will have fish for flesh and simpler cheer. But then the weather of the world chides with winter; the cold withdraws itself, the clouds uplift, and the rain falls in warm showers on the fair plains. Then the flowers come forth, meadows and grove are clad in green, the birds make ready to build, and sing sweetly for solace of the soft summer that follows thereafter. The blossoms bud and blow in the hedgerows rich and rank, and noble notes enough are heard in the fair woods.

TRANSLATED BY JESSIE WESTON

After the season of summer, with the soft winds, when zephyr breathes lightly on seeds and herbs, joyous indeed is the growth that waxes thereout when the dew drips from the leaves beneath the blissful glance of the bright sun. But then comes harvest and hardens the grain, warning it to wax ripe ere the winter. The drought drives the dust on high, flying over the face of the land; the angry wind of the welkin wrestles with the sun; the leaves fall from the trees and light upon the ground, and all brown are the groves that but now were green, and ripe is the fruit that once was flower. So the year passes into many yesterdays, and winter comes again, as it needs no sage to tell us.

SIR GAWAIN BETHINKS HIM OF HIS COVENANT

When the Michaelmas moon was come in with warnings of winter, Sir Gawain bethought him full oft of his perilous journey. Yet till All Hallows Day he lingered with Arthur, and on that day they made a great feast for the hero's sake, with much revel and richness of the Round Table. Courteous knights and comely ladies, all were in sorrow for the love of that knight, and though they spake no word of it, many were joyless for his sake.

And after meat, sadly Sir Gawain turned to his uncle, and spake of his journey, and said, 'Liege lord of my life, leave from you I crave. Ye know well how the matter stands without more words; tomorrow am I bound to set forth in search of the Green Knight.'

Then came together all the noblest knights, Ywain and Erec, and many another. Sir Dodinel le Sauvage, the Duke of Clarence, Launcelot and Lionel, and Lucan the Good, Sir Bors and Sir Bedivere, valiant knights both, and many another hero, with Sir Mador de la Porte, and they all drew near, heavy at heart, to take counsel with Sir Gawain. Much sorrow and weeping was there in the hall to think that so worthy a knight as Gawain should wend his way to seek a deadly blow, and should no more wield his sword in fight. But the knight made ever good cheer, and said, 'Nay, wherefore should I shrink? What may a man do but prove his fate?'

THE ARMING OF SIR GAWAIN

He dwelt there all that day, and on the morn he arose and asked betimes for his armour; and they brought it unto him on this wise: first, a rich carpet was stretched on the floor (and brightly did the gold gear glitter upon it), then the knight stepped on to it, and handled the steel; clad he was in a doublet of silk, with a close hood, lined fairly throughout. Then they set the steel shoes upon his feet, and wrapped his legs with greaves, with polished knee-caps, fastened with knots of gold. Then they cased his thighs in cuisses closed with thongs, and brought him the byrnie of bright steel rings sewn upon a fair stuff. Well burnished braces they set on each arm with good elbow-pieces, and gloves of mail, and all the goodly gear that should shield him in his need. And they cast over all a rich surcoat, and set the golden spurs on his heels, and girt him with a trusty sword fastened with a silken bawdrick. When he was thus clad his harness was costly, for the least loop or latchet gleamed with gold. So armed as he was he hearkened Mass and made his offering at the high altar. Then he came to the king, and the knights of his court, and courteously took leave of lords and ladies, and they kissed him, and commended him to Christ.

With that was Gringalet ready, girt with a saddle that gleamed gaily with many golden fringes, enriched and decked anew for the venture. The bridle was all barred about with bright gold buttons, and all the covertures and trappings of the steed, the crupper and the rich skirts, accorded with the saddle; spread fair with the rich red gold that glittered and gleamed in the rays of the sun.

Then the knight called for his helmet, which was well lined throughout, and set it high on his head, and hasped it behind. He wore a light kerchief over the ventail, that was broidered and studded with fair gems on a broad silken ribbon, with birds of gay color, and many a turtle and true-lover's knot interlaced thickly, even as many a maiden had wrought diligently for seven winter long. But the circlet which crowned his helmet was yet more precious, being adorned with a device in diamonds.

WHEREFORE SIR GAWAIN BARE THE PENTANGLE

Then they brought him his shield, which was of bright red, with the pentangle painted thereon in gleaming gold. And why that noble prince bare the pentangle I am minded to tell you, though my tale tarry thereby. It is a sign that Solomon set ere-while, as betokening truth; for it is a figure with five points and each line overlaps the other, and nowhere hath it beginning or end, so that in English it is called 'the endless knot.' And therefore was it well suiting to this knight and to his arms, since Gawain was faithful in five and five-fold, for pure was he as gold, void of all villainy and endowed with all virtues. Therefore he bare the pentangle on shield and surcoat as truest of heroes and gentlest of knights.

For first he was faultless in his five senses; and his five fingers never failed him; and all his trust upon earth was in the five wounds that Christ bare on the cross, as the Creed tells. And wherever this knight found himself in stress of battle he deemed well that he drew his strength from the five joys which the Queen of Heaven had of her Child. And for this cause did he bear an image of Our Lady on the one half of his shield, that whenever he looked upon it he might not lack for aid. And the fifth five that the hero used were frankness and fellowship above all, purity and courtesy that never failed him, and compassion that surpasses all; and in these five virtues was that hero wrapped and clothed. And all these, five-fold, were linked one in the other, so that they had no end, and were fixed on five points that never failed, neither at any side were they joined or sundered, nor could ye find beginning or end. And therefore on his shield was the knot shapen, red gold upon red, which is the pure pentangle. Now was Sir Gawain ready, and he took his lance in hand, and bade them all Farewell, he deemed it had been for ever.

HOW SIR GAWAIN WENT FORTH

Then he smote the steed with his spurs, and sprang on his way, so that sparks flew from the stones after him. All that saw him were grieved at heart, and said one to the other, 'By Christ, 'tis great pity that one of such noble life should be lost! I' faith, 'twere not easy to find his equal upon earth. The king had done better to have wrought more warily. Yonder knight should have been made a duke; a gallant leader of men is he, and such a fate had beseemed him better than to be hewn in pieces at the will of an elfish man, for mere pride. Who ever knew a king to take such counsel as to risk his knights on a Christmas jest?' Many were the tears that flowed from their eyes when that goodly knight rode from the hall. He made no delaying, but went his way swiftly, and rode many a wild road, as I heard say in the book.

OF SIR GAWAIN'S JOURNEY

So rode Sir Gawain through the realm of Logres, on an errand that he held for no jest. Often he lay companionless at night, and must lack the fare that he liked. No comrade had he save his steed, and none save God with whom to take counsel. At length he drew nigh to North Wales, and left the isles of Anglesey on his left hand, crossing over the fords by the foreland over at Holyhead, till he came into the wilderness of Wirral, where but few dwell who love God and man of true heart. And ever he asked, as he fared, of all whom he met, if they had heard any tidings of a Green Knight in the country thereabout, or of a Green Chapel? And all answered him, Nay, never in their lives had they seen any man of such a hue. And the knight wended his way by many a strange road and many a rugged path, and the fashion of his countenance changed full often ere he saw the Green Chapel.

Many a cliff did he climb in that unknown land, where afar from his friends he rode as a stranger. Never did he come to a stream or a ford but he found a foe before him, and that one so marvelous, so foul and fell, that it behooved him to fight. So many wonders did that knight behold, that it were too long to tell the tenth part of them. Sometimes he fought with dragons and wolves; sometimes with wild men that dwelt in the rocks; another while with bulls, and bears, and wild boars, or with giants of the high moorland that drew near to him. Had he not been a doughty knight, enduring, and of well-proved valour, and a servant of God, doubtless he had been slain, for he was oft in danger of death. Yet he cared not so much for the strife; what he deemed worse was when the cold clear water was shed from the clouds, and froze ere it fell on the fallow ground. More nights than enough he slept in his harness on the bare rocks, near slain with the sleet, while the stream leapt bubbling from the crest of the hills, and hung in hard icicles over his head.

Thus in peril and pain, and many a hardship, the knight rode alone till Christmas Eve, and in that tide he made his prayer to the Blessed Virgin that she would guide his steps and lead him to some dwelling. On that morning he rode by a hill, and came into a thick forest, wild and drear; on each side were high hills, and thick woods below them of great hoar oaks, a hundred together, of hazel and hawthorn with their trailing boughs intertwined, and rough ragged moss spreading everywhere. On the bare twigs the birds chirped piteously, for pain of the cold. The knight upon Gringalet rode lonely beneath them, through marsh and mire, much troubled at heart lest he should fail to see the service of the Lord, who on that self-same night was born of a maiden for the cure of our grief; and therefore he said, sighing, 'I beseech Thee, Lord, and Mary Thy gentle Mother, for some shelter where

I may hear Mass, and Thy matins at morn. This I ask meekly, and thereto I pray my Paternoster, Ave, and Credo.' Thus he rode praying, and lamenting his misdeeds, and he crossed himself, and said, 'May the Cross of Christ speed me.'

HOW SIR GAWAIN CAME TO A FAIR CASTLE ON CHRISTMAS EVE

Now that knight had crossed himself but thrice ere he was aware in the wood of a dwelling within a moat, above a lawn, on a mound surrounded by many mighty trees that stood round the moat. 'Twas the fairest castle that ever a knight owned; built in a meadow with a park all about it, and a spiked palisade, closely driven, that enclosed the trees for more than two miles. The knight was ware of the hold from the side, as it shone through the oaks. Then he lifted off his helmet and thanked Christ and S. Julian that they had courteously granted his prayer, and hearkened to his cry. 'Now,' quoth the knight, 'I beseech ye, grant me fair hostel.' Then he pricked Gringalet with his golden spurs, and rode gaily towards the great gate, and came swiftly to the bridge end.

The bridge was drawn up and the gates close shut; the walls were strong and thick, so that they might fear no tempest. The knight on his charger abode on the bank of the deep double ditch that surrounded the castle. The walls were set deep in the water, and rose aloft to a wondrous height; they were of hard hewn stone up to the corbels, which were adorned beneath the battlements with fair carvings, and turrets set in between with many a loophole; a better barbican Sir Gawain had never looked upon. And within he beheld the high hall, with its tower and many windows with carven cornices, and chalk-white chimneys on the turreted roofs that shone fair in the sun. And everywhere, thickly scattered on the castle battlements, were pinnacles, so many that it seemed as if it were all wrought out of paper, so white was it.

The knight on his steed deemed it fair enough, if he might come to be sheltered within it to lodge there while that the Holy-day lasted. He called aloud, and soon there came a porter of kindly countenance, who stood on the wall and greeted this knight and asked his errand.

'Good sir,' quoth Gawain, 'wilt thou go mine errand to the high lord of the castle, and crave for me lodging?'

'Yea, by S. Peter,' quoth the porter. 'In sooth I trow that ye be welcome to dwell here so long as it may like ye.'

HOW SIR GAWAIN WAS WELCOMED

Then he went, and came again swiftly, and many folk with him to receive the knight. They let down the great drawbridge, and came forth and knelt on their knees on the cold earth to give him worthy welcome. They held wide open the great gates, and courteously he bade them rise, and rode over the bridge. Then men came to him and held his stirrup while he dismounted, and took and stabled his steed. There came down knights and squires to bring the guest with joy to the hall. When he raised his helmet there were many to take it from his hand, fain to serve him, and they took from him sword and shield.

Sir Gawain gave good greeting to the noble and the mighty men who came to do him honour. Clad in his shining armour they led him to the hall, where a great fire burnt brightly on the floor; and the lord of the household came forth from his chamber to meet the hero fitly. He spake to the knight, and said: 'Ye are welcome to do here as it likes ye. All that is here is your own to have at your will and disposal.'

'Gramercy!' quoth Gawain, 'may Christ requite ye.'

As friends that were fain each embraced the other; and Gawain looked on the knight who greeted him so kindly and thought 'twas a bold warrior that owned that burg.

Of mighty stature he was, and of high age; broad and flowing was his beard, and of a bright hue. He was stalwart of limb, and strong in his stride, his face fiery red, and his speech free: in sooth he seemed one well fitted to be a leader of valiant men.

Then the lord led Sir Gawain to a chamber, and

commanded folk to wait upon him, and at his bidding there came men enough who brought the guest to a fair bower. The bedding was noble, with curtains of pure silk wrought with gold, and wondrous coverings of fair cloth all embroidered. The curtains ran on ropes with rings of red gold, and the walls were hung with carpets of Orient, and the same spread on the floor. There with mirthful speeches they took from the guest his byrnie and all his shining armour, and brought him rich robes of the choicest in its stead. They were long and flowing, and became him well, and when he was clad in them all who looked on the hero thought that surely God had never made a fairer knight: he seemed as if he might be a prince without peer in the field where men strive in battle.

Then before the hearth-place, whereon the fire burned, they made ready a chair for Gawain, hung about with cloth and fair cushions; and there they cast around him a mantle of brown samite, richly embroidered and furred within with costly skins of ermine, with a hood of the same, and he seated himself in that rich seat, and warmed himself at the fire, and was cheered at heart. And while he sat thus, the serving men set up a table on trestles, and covered it with a fair white cloth, and set thereon salt cellar, and napkin, and silver spoons; and the knight washed at his will, and set him down to meat.

The folk served him courteously with many dishes seasoned of the best, a double portion. All kinds of fish were there, some baked in bread, some broiled on the embers, some sodden, some stewed and savored with spices, with all sorts of cunning devices to his taste. And often he called it a feast, when they spake gaily to him all together, and said, 'Now take ye this penance, and it shall be for your amendment.' Much mirth thereof did Sir Gawain make.

SIR GAWAIN TELLS HIS NAME

Then they questioned that prince courteously of whence he came; and he told them that he was of the court of Arthur, who is the rich royal king of the Round Table, and that it was Gawain himself who was within their walls, and would keep Christmas with them, as the chance had fallen out. And when the lord of the castle heard those tidings he laughed aloud for gladness, and all men in that keep were joyful that they should be in the company of him to whom belonged all fame, and valour, and courtesy, and whose honour was praised above that of all men on earth. Each said softly to his fellow, 'Now shall we see courteous bearing, and the manner of speech befitting courts. What charm lieth in gentle speech shall we learn without asking, since here we have welcomed the fine father of courtesy. God has surely shewn us his grace since he sends us such a guest as Gawain! When men shall sit and sing, blithe for Christ's birth, this knight shall bring us to the knowledge of fair manners, and it may be that hearing him we may learn the cunning speech of love.'

By the time the knight had risen from dinner it was near nightfall. Then chaplains took their way to the chapel, and rang loudly, even as they should, for the solemn evensong of the high feast. Thither went the lord, and the lady also, and entered with her maidens into a comely closet, and thither also went Gawain. Then the lord took him by the sleeve and led him to a seat, and called him by his name, and told him he was of all men in the world the most welcome. And Sir Gawain thanked him truly, and each kissed the other, and they sat gravely together throughout the service.

THE LADY OF THE CASTLE
Then was the lady fain to look upon that knight; and she came forth from her closet with many fair maidens. The fairest of ladies was she in face, and figure, and coloring, fairer even than Guinevere, so the knight thought. She came through the chancel to greet the hero; another lady held her by the left hand, older than she, and seemingly of high estate, with many nobles about her. But unlike to look upon were those ladies,

for if the younger were fair, the elder was yellow. Rich red were the cheeks of the one, rough and wrinkled those of the other; the kerchiefs of the one were broidered with many glistening pearls, her throat and neck bare, and whiter than the snow that lies on the hills; the neck of the other was swathed in a gorget, with a white wimple over her black chin. Her forehead was wrapped in silk with many folds, worked with knots, so that naught of her was seen save her black brows, her eyes, her nose, and her lips, and those were bleared, and ill to look upon. A worshipful lady in sooth one might call her! In figure was she short and broad, and thickly made – far fairer to behold was she whom she led by the hand.

When Gawain beheld that fair lady, who looked at him graciously, with leave of the lord he went towards them, and, bowing low, he greeted the elder, but the younger and fairer he took lightly in his arms, and kissed her courteously, and greeted her in knightly wise. Then she hailed him as friend, and he quickly prayed to be counted as her servant, if she so willed. Then they took him between them, and talking, led him to the chamber, to the hearth, and bade them bring spices, and they brought them in plenty with the good wine that was wont to be drunk at such seasons. Then the lord sprang to his feet and bade them make merry, and took off his hood, and hung it on a spear, and bade him win the worship thereof who should make most mirth that Christmastide. 'And I shall try, by my faith, to fool it with the best, by the help of my friends, ere I lose my raiment.' Thus with gay words the lord made trial to gladden Gawain with jests that night, till it was time to bid them light the tapers, and Sir Gawain took leave of them and gat him to rest.

OF THE CHRISTMAS FEAST
In the morn when all men call to mind how Christ our Lord was born on earth to die for us, there is joy, for his sake, in all dwellings of the world; and so was there here on that day.

For high feast was held, with many dainties and cunningly cooked messes. On the daïs sat gallant men, clad in their best. The ancient dame sat on the high seat, with the lord of the castle beside her. Gawain and the fair lady sat together, even in the midst of the board when the feast was served; and so throughout all the hall each sat in his degree, and was served in order. There was meat, there was mirth, there was much joy, so that to tell thereof would take me too long, though peradventure I might strive to declare it. But Gawain and that fair lady had much joy of each other's company through her sweet words and courteous converse. And there was music made before each prince, trumpets and drums, and merry piping; each man hearkened his minstrel, and they too hearkened theirs.

HOW THE FEAST CAME TO AN END BUT GAWAIN ABODE AT THE CASTLE

So they held high feast that day and the next, and the third day thereafter, and the joy on S. John's Day was fair to hearken, for 'twas the last of the feast and the guests would depart in the grey of the morning. Therefore they awoke early, and drank wine, and danced fair carols, and at last, when it was late, each man took his leave to wend early on his way. Gawain would bid his host farewell, but the lord took him by the hand, and led him to his own chamber beside the hearth, and there he thanked him for the favour he had shown him in honouring his dwelling at that high season, and gladdening his castle with his fair countenance. 'I wis, sir, that while I live I shall be held the worthier that Gawain has been my guest at God's own feast.'

'Gramercy, sir,' quoth Gawain, 'in good faith, all the honour is yours, may the High King give it you, and I am but at your will to work your behest, inasmuch as I am beholden to you in great and small by rights.'

Then the lord did his best to persuade the knight to tarry

with him, but Gawain answered that he might in no wise do so. Then the host asked him courteously what stern behest had driven him at the holy season from the king's court, to fare all alone, ere yet the feast was ended?

'Forsooth,' quoth the knight, 'ye say but the truth: 'tis a high quest and a pressing that hath brought me afield, for I am summoned myself to a certain place, and I know not whither in the world I may wend to find it; so help me Christ, I would give all the kingdom of Logres an I might find it by New Year's morn. Therefore, sir, I make request of you that ye tell me truly if ye ever heard word of the Green Chapel, where it may be found, and the Green Knight that keeps it. For I am pledged by solemn compact sworn between us to meet that knight at the New Year if so I were on life; and of that same New Year it wants but little – 'I faith, I would look on that hero more joyfully than on any other fair sight! Therefore, by your will, it behooves me to leave you, for I have but barely three days, and I would as fain fall dead as fall of mine errand.'

Then the lord quoth, laughing, 'Now must ye needs stay, for I will show you your goal, the Green Chapel, ere your term be at an end, have ye no fear! But ye can take your ease, friend, in your bed, till the fourth day, and go forth on the first of the year and come to that place at mid-morn to do as ye will. Dwell here till New Year's Day, and then rise and set forth, and ye shall be set in the way; 't is not two miles hence.'

Then was Gawain glad, and he laughed gaily: 'Now I thank you for this above all else. Now my quest is achieved I will dwell here at your will, and otherwise do as ye shall ask.'

Then the lord took him, and set him beside him, and bade the ladies be fetched for their greater pleasure, though between themselves they had solace. The lord, for gladness, made merry jest, even as one who wist not what to do for joy; and he cried aloud to the knight, 'Ye have promised to do the thing I bid ye: will ye hold to this behest, here, at once?'

'Yea, forsooth,' said that true knight, 'while I abide in your burg I am bound by your behest.'

'Ye have traveled from far,' said the host, 'and since then ye have waked with me, ye are not well refreshed by rest and sleep, as I know. Ye shall therefore abide in your chamber, and lie at your ease tomorrow at Mass-tide, and go to meat when ye will with my wife, who shall sit with you, and comfort you with her company till I return; and I shall rise early and go forth to the chase.' And Gawain agreed to all this courteously.

SIR GAWAIN MAKES A COVENANT WITH HIS HOST

'Sir knight,' quoth the host, 'we will make a covenant. Whatsoever I win in the wood shall be yours, and whatever may fall to your share, that shall ye exchange for it. Let us swear, friend, to make this exchange, however our hap may be, for worse or for better.'

'I grant ye your will,' quoth Gawain the good; 'if ye list so to do, it liketh me well.'

'Bring hither the wine-cup, the bargain is made,' so said the lord of that castle. They laughed each one, and drank of the wine, and made merry, these lords and ladies, as it pleased them. Then with gay talk and merry test they arose, and stood, and spoke softly, and kissed courteously, and took leave of each other. With burning torches, and many a serving-man, was each led to his couch; yet ere they gat them to bed the old lord oft repeated their covenant, for he knew well how to make sport.

BOOK III

THE FIRST DAY'S HUNTING
Full early, ere daylight, the folk rose up; the guests who would depart called their grooms, and they made them ready, and saddled the steeds, tightened up the girths, and trussed up their mails. The knights, all arrayed for riding, leapt up lightly, and took their bridles, and each rode his way as pleased him best.

The lord of the land was not the last. Ready for the chase, with many of his men, he ate a sop hastily when he had heard Mass, and then with blast of the bugle fared forth to the field. He and his nobles were to horse ere daylight glimmered upon the earth.

Then the huntsmen coupled their hounds, unclosed the kennel door, and called them out. They blew three blasts gaily on the bugles, the hounds bayed fiercely, and they that would go a-hunting checked and chastised them. A hundred hunters there were of the best, so I have heard tell. Then the trackers gat them to the trysting-place and uncoupled the hounds, and the forest rang again with their gay blasts.

At the first sound of the hunt the game quaked for fear, and fled, trembling, along the vale. They betook them to the heights, but the liers in wait turned them back with loud cries; the harts they let pass them, and the stags with their spreading antlers, for the lord had forbidden that they should be slain, but the hinds and the does they turned back, and drave down into the valleys. Then might ye see much shooting of arrows. As the deer fled under the boughs a broad whistling shaft smote and wounded each sorely, so that, wounded and bleeding, they fell dying on the banks. The hounds followed swiftly on their tracks, and hunters, blowing the horn, sped after them with ringing shouts as if the cliffs burst asunder. What game escaped those that shot was run down at the outer ring. Thus were they driven on the hills, and harassed at the waters, so well did the men know their work, and the greyhounds were so great and swift that they rail them down as fast as the hunters could slay them. Thus the lord passed the day in mirth and joyfulness, even to nightfall.

HOW THE LADY OF THE CASTLE CAME TO SIR GAWAIN
So the lord roamed the woods, and Gawain, that good night, lay ever a-bed, curtained about, under the costly coverlet, while the daylight gleamed on the walls. And as he lay half slumbering, he heard a little sound at the door, and he raised his head, and caught back a corner of the curtain, and waited to see what it might be. It was the lovely lady, the lord's wife; she shut the door softly behind her, and turned towards the bed; and Gawain was shamed, laid him down softly and made as if he slept. And she came lightly to the bedside, within the curtain, and sat herself down beside him, to wait till he wakened. The knight lay there awhile, and marveled within himself what her coming might betoken; and he said to himself, "Twere more seemly if I asked her what hath brought her hither.' Then he made feint to waken, and turned towards her, and opened his eyes as one astonished, and crossed himself; and she looked on him laughing, with her cheeks red and white, lovely to behold, and small smiling lips.

'Good morrow, Sir Gawain,' said that fair lady; 'ye are but a careless sleeper, since one can enter thus. Now are ye

SIR GAWAIN AND THE GREEN KNIGHT

taken unawares, and lest ye escape me I shall bind you in your bed; of that be ye assured!' Laughing, she spake these words.

'Good morrow, fair lady,' quoth Gawain blithely. 'I will do your will, as it likes me well. For I yield me readily, and pray your grace, and that is best, by my faith, since I needs must do so.' Thus he jested again, laughing. 'But an ye would, fair lady, grant me this grace that ye pray your prisoner to rise. I would get me from bed, and array me better, then could I talk with ye in more comfort.'

'Nay, forsooth, fair sir,' quoth the lady, 'ye shall not rise, I will rede ye better. I shall keep ye here, since ye can do no other, and talk with my knight whom I have captured. For I know well that ye are Sir Gawain, whom all the world worships, wheresoever ye may ride. Your honour and your courtesy are praised by lords and ladies, by all who live. Now ye are here and we are alone, my lord and his men are afield; the serving men in their beds, and my maidens also, and the door shut upon us. And since in this hour I have him that all men love, I shall use my time well with speech, while it lasts. Ye are welcome to my company, for it behoves me in sooth to be your servant.'

'In good faith,' quoth Gawain, 'I think me that I am not him of whom ye speak, for unworthy am I of such service as ye here proffer. In sooth, I were glad if I might set myself by word or service to your pleasure; a pure joy would it be to me!'

'In good faith, Sir Gawain,' quoth the gay lady, 'the praise and the prowess that pleases all ladies I lack them not, nor hold them light; yet are there ladies enough who would liever now have the knight in their hold, as I have ye here, to dally with your courteous words, to bring them comfort and to ease their cares, than much of the treasure and the gold that are theirs. And now, through the grace of Him who upholds the heavens, I have wholly in my power that which they all desire!'

Thus the lady, fair to look upon, made him great cheer, and Sir Gawain, with modest words, answered her again: 'Madam,' he quoth, 'may Mary requite ye, for in good faith

I have found in ye a noble frankness. Much courtesy have other folk shown me, but the honour they have done me is naught to the worship of yourself, who knoweth but good.'

'By Mary,' quoth the lady, 'I think otherwise; for were I worth all the women alive, and had I the wealth of the world in my hand, and might choose me a lord to my liking, then, for all that I have seen in ye, Sir Knight, of beauty and courtesy and blithe semblance, and for all that I have hearkened and hold for true, there should be no knight on earth to be chosen before ye!'

'Well I wot,' quoth Sir Gawain, 'that ye have chosen a better; but I am proud that ye should so prize me, and as your servant do I hold ye my sovereign, and your knight am I, and may Christ reward ye.'

So they talked of many matters till mid-morn was past, and ever the lady made as though she loved him, and the knight turned her speech aside. For though she were the brightest of maidens, yet had he forborne to show her love for the danger that awaited him, and the blow that must be given without delay.

Then the lady prayed her leave from him, and he granted it readily. And she gave him good day, with laughing glance, but he must needs marvel at her words:

'Now He that speeds fair speech reward ye this disport; but that ye be Gawain my mind misdoubts me greatly.'

'Wherefore?' quoth the knight quickly, fearing lest he had lacked in some courtesy.

And the lady spake: 'So true a knight as Gawain is holden, and one so perfect in courtesy, would never have tarried so long with a lady but he would of his courtesy have craved a kiss at parting.'

HOW THE LADY KISSED SIR GAWAIN

Then quoth Gawain, 'I wot I will do even as it may please ye, and kiss at your commandment, as a true knight should who forbears to ask for fear of displeasure.'

SIR GAWAIN AND THE GREEN KNIGHT

At that she came near and bent down and kissed the knight, and each commended the other to Christ, and she went forth from the chamber softly.

Then Sir Gawain arose and called his chamberlain and chose his garments, and when he was ready he gat him forth to Mass, and then went to meat, and made merry all day till the rising of the moon, and never had a knight fairer lodging than had he with those two noble ladies, the elder and the younger.

And ever the lord of the land chased the hinds through holt and heath till eventide, and then with much blowing of bugles and baying of hounds they bore the game homeward; and by the time daylight was done all the folk had returned to that fair castle. And when the lord and Sir Gawain met together, then were they both well pleased. The lord commanded them all to assemble in the great hall, and the ladies to descend with their maidens, and there, before them all, he bade the men fetch in the spoil of the day's hunting, and he called unto Gawain, and counted the tale of the beasts, and showed them unto him, and said, 'What think ye of this game, Sir Knight? Have I deserved of ye thanks for my woodcraft?'

'Yea, I wis,' quoth the other, 'here is the fairest spoil I have seen this seven year in the winter season.'

HOW THE COVENANT WAS KEPT

'And all this do I give ye, Gawain,' quoth the host, 'for by accord of covenant ye may claim it as your own.'

'That is sooth,' quoth the other, 'I grant you that same; and I have fairly won this within walls, and with as good will do I yield it to ye.' With that he clasped his hands round the lord's neck and kissed him as courteously as he might. 'Take ye here my spoils, no more have I won; ye should have it freely, though it were greater than this.'

''Tis good,' said the host, 'gramercy thereof. Yet were I fain to know where ye won this same favour, and if it were by your own wit?'

'Nay,' answered Gawain, 'that was not in the bond. Ask me no more: ye have taken what was yours by right, be content with that.'

They laughed and jested together, and sat them down to supper, where they were served with many dainties; and after supper they sat by the hearth, and wine was served out to them; and oft in their jesting they promised to observe on the morrow the same covenant that they had made before, and whatever chance might betide, to exchange their spoil, be it much or little, when they met at night. Thus they renewed their bargain before the whole court, and then the night-drink was served, and each courteously took leave of the other and gat him to bed.

ON THE SECOND DAY'S HUNTING

By the time the cock had crowed thrice the lord of the castle had left his bed; Mass was sung and meat fitly served. The folk were forth to the wood ere the day broke, with hound and horn they rode over the plain, and uncoupled their dogs among the thorns. Soon they struck on the scent, and the hunt cheered on the hounds who were first to seize it, urging them with shouts. The others hastened to the cry, forty at once, and there rose such a clamour from the pack that the rocks rang again. The huntsman spurred them on with shouting and blasts of the horn; and the hounds drew together to a thicket betwixt the water and a high crag in the cliff beneath the hillside. There where the rough rock fell ruggedly they, the huntsmen, fared to the finding, and cast about round the hill and the thicket behind them. The knights wist well what beast was within, and would drive him forth with the bloodhounds. And as they beat the bushes, suddenly over the beaters there rushed forth a wondrous great and fierce boar, long since had he left the herd to roam by himself. Grunting, he cast many to the ground, and fled forth at his best speed, without more mischief. The men hallooed loudly and cried, '*Hay! Hay!*' and blew the horns to urge on the hounds, and rode swiftly after the boar. Many a time did he turn to bay and tare the hounds, and they yelped, and howled shrilly. Then the men made ready their arrows and shot at him, but the points were turned on his thick hide, and the barbs would not bite upon him, for the shafts shivered in pieces, and the head but leapt again wherever it hit.

But when the boar felt the stroke of the arrows he waxed mad with rage, and turned on the hunters and tare many, so that, affrightened, they fled before him. But the lord on a swift steed pursued him, blowing his bugle; as a gallant knight he rode through the woodland chasing the boar till the sun grew low.

So did the hunters this day, while Sir Gawain lay in his bed lapped in rich gear; and the lady forgat not to salute him, for early was she at his side, to cheer his mood.

OF THE LADY AND SIR GAWAIN

She came to the bedside and looked on the knight, and Gawain gave her fit greeting, and she greeted him again with ready words, and sat her by his side and laughed, and with a sweet look she spoke to him:

'Sir, if ye be Gawain, I think it a wonder that ye be so stern and cold, and care not for the courtesies of friendship, but if one teach ye to know them ye cast the lesson out of your mind. Ye have soon forgotten what I taught ye yesterday, by all the truest tokens that I knew!'

'What is that?' quoth the knight. 'I trow I know not. If it be sooth that ye say, then is the blame mine own.'

'But I taught ye of kissing,' quoth the fair lady. 'Wherever a fair countenance is shown him, it behooves a courteous knight quickly to claim a kiss.'

'Nay, my dear,' said Sir Gawain, 'cease that speech; that durst I not do lest I were denied, for if I were forbidden I wot I were wrong did I further entreat.'

'I' faith,' quoth the lady merrily, 'ye may not be forbid, ye are strong enough to constrain by strength an ye will, were any so discourteous as to give ye denial.'

'Yes, by Heaven,' said Gawain, 'ye speak well; but threats profit little in the land where I dwell, and so with a gift that is given not of good will! I am at your commandment to kiss when ye like, to take or to leave as ye list.'

Then the lady bent her down and kissed him courteously.

HOW THE LADY STROVE TO BEGUILE SIR GAWAIN WITH WORDS OF LOVE

And as they spake together she said, 'I would learn somewhat from ye, an ye would not be wroth, for young ye bare and fair, and so courteous and knightly as ye are known to be, the head of all chivalry, and versed in all wisdom of love and war – 'tis ever told of true knights how they adventured their lives for their true love, and endured hardships for her favours, and avenged her with valour, and eased her sorrows, and brought joy to her bower; and ye are the fairest knight of your time, and your fame and your honour are everywhere, yet I have sat by ye here twice, and never a word have I heard of love! Ye who are so courteous and skilled in such love ought surely to teach one so young and unskilled some little craft of true love! Why are ye so unlearned who art otherwise so famous? Or is it that ye deemed me unworthy to hearken to your teaching? For shame, Sir Knight! I come hither alone and sit at your side to learn of ye some skill; teach me of your wit, while my lord is from home.'

'In good faith,' quoth Gawain, 'great is my joy and my profit that so fair a lady as ye are should deign to come hither, and trouble ye with so poor a man, and make sport with your knight with kindly countenance, it pleaseth me much. But that I, in my turn, should take it upon me to tell of love and such like matters to ye who know more by half, or a hundred fold, of such craft than I do, or ever shall in all my lifetime, by my troth 'twere folly indeed! I will work your will to the best of my might as I am bounden, and evermore will I be your servant, so help me Christ!'

Then often with guile she questioned that knight that

she might win him to woo her, but he defended himself so fairly that none might in any wise blame him, and naught but bliss and harmless jesting was there between them. They laughed and talked together till at last she kissed him, and craved her leave of him, and went her way.

Then the knight arose and went forth to Mass, and afterward dinner was served and he sat and spake with the ladies all day. But the lord of the castle rode ever over the land chasing the wild boar, that fled through the thickets, slaying the best of his hounds and breaking their backs in sunder; till at last he was so weary he might run no longer, be made for a hole in a mound by a rock. He got the mound at his back and faced the hounds, whetting his white tusks and foaming at the mouth. The huntsmen stood aloof, fearing to draw nigh him; so many of them had been already wounded that they were loath to be torn with his tusks, so fierce he was and mad with rage.

HOW THE BOAR WAS SLAIN

At length the lord himself came up, and saw the beast at bay, and the men standing aloof. Then quickly he sprang to the ground and drew out a bright blade, and waded through the stream to the boar.

When the beast was aware of the knight with weapon in hand, he set up his bristles and snorted loudly, and many feared for their lord lest he should be slain. Then the boar leapt upon the knight so that beast and man were one atop of the other in the water; but the boar had the worst of it, for the man had marked, even as he sprang, and set the point of his brand to the beast's chest, and drove it up to the hilt, so that the heart was split in twain, and the boar fell snarling, and was swept down by the water to where a hundred hounds seized on him, and the men drew him to shore for the dogs to slay.

Then was there loud blowing of horns and baying of hounds, the huntsmen smote off the boar's head, and hung the carcass by the four feet to a stout pole, and so went on their way homewards. The head they bore before the lord himself, who had slain the beast at the ford by force of his strong hand.

It seemed him o'er long ere he saw Sir Gawain in the hall, and he called, and the guest came to take that which fell to his share. And when he saw Gawain the lord laughed aloud, and bade them call the ladies and the household together, and he showed them the game, and told them the tale, how they hunted the wild boar through the woods, and of his length and breadth and height; and Sir Gawain commended his deeds and praised him for his valour, well proven, for so mighty a beast had he never seen before.

THE KEEPING OF THE COVENANT
Then they handled the huge head, and the lord said aloud, 'Now, Gawain, this game is your own by sure covenant, as ye right well know.'

"Tis sooth,' quoth the knight, 'and as truly will I give ye all I have gained.' He took the host round the neck, and kissed him courteously twice. 'Now are we quits,' he said, 'this eventide, of all the covenants that we made since I came hither.'

And the lord answered, 'By S. Giles, ye are the best I know; ye will be rich in a short space if ye drive such bargains!'

Then they set up the tables on trestles and covered them with fair cloths, and lit waxen tapers on the walls. The knights sat and were served in the hall and much game and glee was there round the hearth, with many songs, both at supper and after; song of Christmas, and new carols, with all the mirth one may think of. And ever that lovely lady sat by the knight, and with still stolen looks made such feint of pleasing him, that Gawain marveled much and was wroth with himself, but he could not for his courtesy return her fair glances, but dealt with her cunningly, however she might strive to wrest the thing.

When they had tarried in the hall so long as it seemed them good, they turned to the inner chamber and the wide hearth-place, and there they drank wine, and the host proffered to renew the covenant for New Year's Eve; but the knight craved leave to depart on the morrow, for it was nigh to the term when he must fulfil his pledge. But the lord would withhold him from so doing, and prayed him to tarry, and said,

'As I am a true knight I swear my troth that ye shall come to the Green Chapel to achieve your task on New Year's morn, long before prime. Therefore abide ye in your bed, and I will hunt in this wood, and hold ye to the covenant to exchange with me against all the spoil I may bring hither. For twice have I tried ye, and found ye true, and the morrow shall be the third time and the best. Make we merry now while we may, and think on joy, for misfortune may take a man whensoever it wills.'

Then Gawain granted his request, and they brought them drink, and they gat them with lights to bed.

OF THE THIRD DAY'S HUNTING

Sir Gawain lay and slept softly, but the lord, who was keen on woodcraft, was afoot early. After Mass he and his men ate a morsel, and he asked for his steed; all the knights who should ride with him were already mounted before the hall gates.

'Twas a fair frosty morning, for the sun rose red in ruddy vapour, and the welkin was clear of clouds. The hunters scattered them by the forest side, and the rocks rang again with the blast of their horns. Some came on the scent of a fox, and a hound gave tongue; the huntsmen shouted, and the pack followed in a crowd on the trail. The fox ran before them, and when they saw him they pursued him with noise and much shouting, and he wound and turned through many a thick grove, often cowering and hearkening in a hedge. At last by a little ditch he leapt out of a spinney, stole away slily by a copse path, and so out of the wood and away from the hounds. But he went, ere he wist, to a chosen tryst, and three started forth on him at once, so he must needs double back, and betake him to the wood again.

Then was it joyful to hearken to the hounds; when all the pack had met together and had sight of their game they made as loud a din as if all the lofty cliffs had fallen clattering together. The huntsmen shouted and threatened, and followed close upon him so that he might scarce escape, but Reynard was wily, and he turned and doubled upon them, and led the lord and his men over the hills, now on the slopes, now in the vales, while the knight at home slept through the cold morning beneath his costly curtains.

HOW THE LADY CAME FOR THE THIRD TIME TO SIR GAWAIN

But the fair lady of the castle rose betimes, and clad herself in a rich mantle that reached even to the ground, left her throat and her fair neck bare, and was bordered and lined with costly furs. On her head she wore no golden circlet, but a network of precious stones, that gleamed and shone through her tresses in clusters of twenty together. Thus she came into the chamber, closed the door after her, and set open a window, and called to him gaily, 'Sir Knight, how may ye sleep? The morning is so fair.'

Sir Gawain was deep in slumber, and in his dream he vexed him much for the destiny that should befall him on the morrow, when he should meet the knight at the Green Chapel, and abide his blow; but when the lady spake he heard her, and came to himself, and roused from his dream and answered swiftly. The lady came laughing, and kissed him courteously, and he welcomed her fittingly with a cheerful countenance. He saw her so glorious and gaily dressed, so faultless of features and complexion, that it warmed his heart to look upon her.

They spake to each other smiling, and all was bliss and good cheer between them. They exchanged fair words, and much happiness was therein, yet was there a gulf between them, and she might win no more of her knight, for that gallant prince watched well his words – he would neither take her love, nor frankly refuse it. He cared for his courtesy, lest he be deemed churlish, and yet more for his honour lest he be traitor to his host. 'God forbid,' quoth he to himself, 'that it should so befall.' Thus with courteous words did he set aside all the special speeches that came from her lips.

Then spake the lady to the knight, 'Ye deserve blame if ye hold not that lady who sits beside ye above all else in the world, if ye have not already a love whom ye hold dearer, and like better, and have sworn such firm faith to that lady that ye care not to loose it – and that am I now fain to believe. And now I pray ye straitly that ye tell me that in truth, and hide it not.'

And the knight answered, 'By S. John' (and he smiled as he spake) 'no such love have I, nor do I think to have yet awhile.'

'That is the worst word I may hear,' quoth the lady, 'but in sooth I have mine answer; kiss me now courteously, and I will go hence; I can but mourn as a maiden that loves much.'

THE LADY WOULD FAIN HAVE A PARTING GIFT FROM GAWAIN

Sighing, she stooped down and kissed him, and then she rose up and spake as she stood, 'Now, dear, at our parting do me this grace: give me some gift, if it were but thy glove, that I may bethink me of my knight, and lessen my mourning.'

'Now, I wis,' quoth the knight, 'I would that I had here the most precious thing that I possess on earth that I might leave ye as love token, great or small, for ye have deserved forsooth more reward than I might give ye. But it is not to your honour to have at this time a glove for reward as gift from Gawain, and I am here on a strange errand, and have no man with me, nor mails with goodly things – that mislikes me much, lady, at this time; but each man must fare as he is taken, if for sorrow and ill.'

SHE WOULD GIVE HIM HER RING

'Nay, knight highly honoured,' quoth that lovesome lady, 'though I have naught of yours, yet shall ye have somewhat of mine.' With that she reached him a ring of red gold with a sparkling stone therein, that shone even as the sun (wit ye well, it was worth many marks); but the knight refused it, and spake readily.

'I will take no gift, lady, at this time. I have none to give, and none will I take.'

She prayed him to take it, but he refused her prayer, and sware in sooth that he would not have it.

ON HER GIRDLE
The lady was sorely vexed, and said, 'If ye refuse my ring as too costly, that ye will not be so highly beholden to me, I will give you my girdle as a lesser gift.' With that she loosened a lace that was fastened at her side, knit upon her kirtle under her mantle. It was wrought of green silk, and gold, only braided by the fingers, and that she offered to the knight, and besought him though it were of little worth that he would take it, and he said nay, he would touch neither gold nor gear ere God give him grace to achieve the adventure for which he had come hither. 'And therefore, I pray ye, displease ye not, and ask me no longer, for I may not grant it. I am dearly beholden to ye for the favour ye have shown me, and ever, in heat and cold, will I be your true servant.'

THE VIRTUE OF THE GIRDLE
'Now,' said the lady, 'ye refuse this silk, for it is simple in itself, and so it seems, indeed; lo, it is small to look upon and less in cost, but whoso knew the virtue that is knit therein he would, peradventure, value it more highly. For whatever knight is girded with this green lace, while he bears it knotted about him there is no man under heaven can overcome him, for he may not be slain for any magic on earth.'

Then Gawain bethought him, and it came into his heart that this were a jewel for the jeopardy that awaited him when he came to the Green Chapel to seek the return blow – could he so order it that he should escape unslain, 'twere a craft worth trying.

HOW SIR GAWAIN TOOK THE GIRDLE
Then he bare with her chiding, and let her say her say, and she pressed the girdle on him and prayed him to take it, and he granted her prayer, and she gave it him with good will, and besought him for her sake never to reveal it but to hide it loyally from her lord; and the knight agreed that never should any man know it, save they two alone. He thanked her often and heartily, and she kissed him for the third time.

Then she took her leave of him, and when she was gone Sir Gawain arose, and clad him in rich attire, and took the girdle, and knotted it round him, and hid it beneath his robes. Then he took his way to the chapel, and sought out a priest privily and prayed him to teach him better how his soul might be saved when he should go hence; and there he shrived him, and showed his misdeeds, both great and small, and besought mercy and craved absolution; and the priest assoiled him, and set him as clean as if doomsday had been on the morrow. And afterwards Sir Gawain made him merry with the ladies, with carols, and all kinds of joy, as never he did but that one day, even to nightfall; and all the men marveled at him, and said that never since he came thither had he been so merry.

THE DEATH OF THE FOX
Meanwhile the lord of the castle was abroad chasing the fox; awhile he lost him, and as he rode through a spinny he heard the hounds near at hand, and Reynard came creeping through a thick grove, with all the pack at his heels. Then the lord drew out his shining brand, and cast it at the beast, and the fox swerved aside for the sharp edge, and would have doubled back, but a hound was on him ere he might turn, and right before the horse's feet they all fell on him, and worried him fiercely, snarling the while.

Then the lord leapt from his saddle, and caught the fox from the jaws, and held it aloft over his head, and hallooed loudly, and many brave hounds bayed as they beheld it; and the hunters hied them thither, blowing their horns; all that bare bugles blew them at once, and all the others shouted. 'Twas the merriest meeting that ever men heard, the clamour that was raised at the death of the fox. They rewarded the hounds, stroking them and rubbing their heads, and took Reynard and stripped him of his coat; then blowing their horns, they turned them homewards, for it was nigh nightfall.

The lord was gladsome at his return, and found a bright fire on the hearth, and the knight beside it, the good Sir Gawain, who was in joyous mood for the pleasure he had had with the ladies. He wore a robe of blue, that reached even to the ground, and a surcoat richly furred, that became him well. A hood like to the surcoat fell on his shoulders, and all alike were done about with fur.

HOW SIR GAWAIN KEPT NOT ALL THE COVENANT

He met the host in the midst of the floor, and jesting, he greeted him, and said, 'Now shall I be first to fulfil our covenant which we made together when there was no lack of wine.' Then he embraced the knight, and kissed him thrice, as solemnly as he might.

'Of a sooth,' quoth the other, 'ye have good luck in the matter of this covenant, if ye made a good exchange.'

'Yea, it matters naught of the exchange,' quoth Gawain, 'since what I owe is swiftly paid.'

'Marry,' said the other, 'mine is behind, for I have hunted all this day, and naught have I got but this foul fox-skin, and that is but poor payment for three such kisses as ye have here given me.'

'Enough,' quoth Sir Gawain, 'I thank ye, by the Rood.'

Then the lord told them of his hunting, and how the fox had been slain.

With mirth and minstrelsy, and dainties at their will, they made them as merry as a folk well might till 'twas time for them to sever, for at last they must needs betake them to their beds. Then the knight took his leave of the lord, and thanked him fairly.

'For the fair sojourn that I have had here at this high feast may the High King give ye honour. I give ye myself, as one of your servants, if ye so like; for I must needs, as you know, go hence with the morn, and ye will give me, as ye promised, a guide to show me the way to the Green Chapel, an God will suffer me on New Year's Day to deal the doom of my weird.'

'By my faith,' quoth the host, 'all that ever I promised, that shall I keep with good will.' Then he gave him a servant to set him in the way, and lead him by the downs, that he should have no need to ford the stream, and should fare by the shortest road through the groves; and Gawain thanked the lord for the honour done him.

HOW SIR GAWAIN TOOK LEAVE OF HIS HOST

Then he would take leave of the ladies, and courteously he kissed them, and spake, praying them to receive his thanks, and they made like reply; then with many sighs they commended him to Christ, and he departed courteously from that folk. Each man that he met he thanked him for his service and his solace, and the pains he had been at to do his will; and each found it as hard to part from the knight as if he had ever dwelt with him.

Then they led him with torches to his chamber, and brought him to his bed to rest. That he slept soundly I may not say, for the morrow gave him much to think on. Let him rest awhile, for he was near that which he sought, and if ye will but listen to me I will tell ye how it fared with him thereafter.

BOOK IV

Now the New Year drew nigh, and the night passed, and the day chased the darkness, as is God's will; but wild weather wakened therewith. The clouds cast the cold to the earth, with enough of the north to slay them that lacked clothing. The snow drave smartly, and the whistling wind blew from the heights, and made great drifts in the valleys. The knight, lying in his bed, listened, for though his eyes were shut, he might sleep but little, and hearkened every cock that crew.

He arose ere the day broke, by the light of a lamp that burned in his chamber, and called to his chamberlain, bidding him bring his armour and saddle his steed. The other gat him up, and fetched his garments, and robed Sir Gawain.

THE ROBING OF SIR GAWAIN
First he clad him in his clothes to keep off the cold, and then in his harness, which was well and fairly kept. Both hauberk and plates were well burnished, the rings of the rich byrny freed from rust, and all as fresh as at first, so that the knight was fain to thank them. Then he did on each piece, and bade them bring his steed, while he put the fairest raiment on himself; his coat with its fair cognizance, adorned with precious stones upon velvet, with broidered seams, and all

furred within with costly skins. And he left not the lace, the lady's gift, that Gawain forgot not, for his own good. When he had girded on his sword he wrapped the gift twice about him, swathed around his waist. The girdle of green silk set gaily and well upon the royal red cloth, rich to behold, but the knight ware it not for pride of the pendants, polished though they were with fair gold that gleamed brightly on the ends, but to save himself from sword and knife, when it behooved him to abide his hurt without question. With that the hero went forth, and thanked that kindly folk full often.

Then was Gringalet ready, that was great and strong, and had been well cared for and tended in every wise; in fair condition was that proud steed, and fit for a journey. Then Gawain went to him, and looked on his coat, and said by his sooth, 'There is a folk in this place that thinketh on honour; much joy may they have, and the lord who maintains them, and may all good betide that lovely lady all her life long. Since they for charity cherish a guest, and hold honour in their hands, may He who holds the heaven on high requite them, and also ye all. And if I might live anywhile on earth, I would give ye full reward, readily, if so I might.'

HOW SIR GAWAIN WENT FORTH FROM THE CASTLE

Then he set foot in the stirrup and bestrode his steed, and his squire gave him his shield, which he laid on his shoulder. Then he smote Gringalet with his golden spurs, and the steed pranced on the stones and would stand no longer.

By that his man was mounted, to bare his spear and lance, and Gawain quoth, 'I commend this castle to Christ, may He give it ever good fortune.' Then the drawbridge was let down, and the broad gates unbarred and opened on both sides; the knight crossed himself, and passed through the gateway, and praised the porter, who knelt before the prince, and gave him good-day, and commended him to God. Thus the knight went on his way with the one man who should

SIR GAWAIN AND THE GREEN KNIGHT

guide him to that dread place where he should receive rueful payment.

The two went by hedges where the boughs were bare, and climbed the cliffs where the cold clings. Naught fell from the heavens, but 'twas ill beneath them; mist brooded over the moor and hung on the mountains; each hill had a cap, a great cloak, of mist. The streams foamed and bubbled between their banks, dashing sparkling on the shores where they shelved downwards. Rugged and dangerous was the way through the woods, till it was time for the sun-rising. Then were they on a high hill; the snow lay white beside them, and the man who rode with Gawain drew rein by his master.

THE SQUIRE'S WARNING

'Sir,' he said, I have brought ye hither, and now ye are not far from the place that ye have sought so specially. But I will tell ye for sooth, since I know ye well, and ye are such a knight as I well love, would ye follow my counsel ye would fare the better.

OF THE KNIGHT OF THE GREEN CHAPEL

'The place whither ye go is accounted full perilous, for he who liveth in that waste is the worst on earth, for he is strong and fierce, and loveth to deal mighty blows; taller he is than any man on earth, and greater of frame than any four in Arthur's court, or in any other. And this is his custom at the Green Chapel; there may no man pass by that place, however proud his arms, but he does him to death by force of his hand, for he is a discourteous knight, and shows no mercy. Be he churl or chaplain who rides by that chapel, monk or mass-priest, or any man else, he thinks it as pleasant to slay them as to pass alive himself. Therefore, I tell ye, as sooth as ye sit in saddle, if ye come there and that knight know it, ye shall be slain, though ye had twenty lives; trow me that truly! He has dwelt here full long and seen many a combat; ye may not defend ye against his blows. Therefore, good Sir Gawain, let the man be, and get ye away some other road; for God's sake seek ye another land, and there may Christ speed ye! And I will hie me home again, and I promise ye further that I will swear by God and the saints, or any other oath ye please, that I will keep counsel faithfully, and never let any wit the tale that ye fled for fear of any man.'

SIR GAWAIN IS NOT DISMAYED

'Gramercy,' quoth Gawain, but ill-pleased. 'Good fortune be his who wishes me good, and that thou wouldst keep faith with me I will believe; but didst thou keep it never so truly, an I passed here and fled for fear as thou sayest, then were I a coward knight, and might not be held guiltless. So I will to the chapel let chance what may, and talk with that man, even as I may list, whether for weal or for woe as fate may have it. Fierce though he may be in fight, yet God knoweth well how to save His servants.'

'Well,' quoth the other, 'now that ye have said so much that ye will take your own harm on yourself, and ye be pleased to lose your life, I will neither let nor keep ye. Have here your helm and the spear in your hand, and ride down this same road beside the rock till ye come to the bottom of the valley, and there look a little to the left hand, and ye shall see in that vale the chapel, and the grim man who keeps it. Now fare ye well, noble Gawain; for all the gold on earth I would not go with ye nor bear ye fellowship one step further.' With that the man turned his bridle into the wood, smote the horse with his spurs as hard as he could, and galloped off, leaving the knight alone.

Quoth Gawain, 'I will neither greet nor groan, but commend myself to God, and yield me to His will.'

Then the knight spurred Gringalet, and rode adown the path close in by a bank beside a grove. So he rode through the rough thicket, right into the dale, and there he halted, for it seemed him wild enough. No sign of a chapel could he see, but high and burnt banks on either side and rough ragged crags with great stones above. An ill-looking place he thought it.

Then he drew in his horse and looked around to seek the chapel, but he saw none and thought it strange. Then he saw as it were a mound on a level space of land by a bank beside the stream where it ran swiftly; the water bubbled within as if boiling. The knight turned his steed to the mound, and lighted down and tied the rein to the branch of a linden; and he turned to the mound and walked round it, questioning with himself what it might be. It had a hole at the end and at either side, and was overgrown with clumps of grass, and it was hollow within as an old cave or the crevice of a crag; he knew not what it might be.

THE FINDING OF THE CHAPEL

'Ah,' quoth Gawain, 'can this be the Green Chapel? Here might the devil say his matins at midnight! Now I wis there is wizardry here. 'Tis an ugly oratory, all overgrown with grass, and 'twould well beseem that fellow in green to say his devotions on devil's wise. Now feel I in five wits, 'tis the foul fiend himself who hath set me this tryst, to destroy me here! This is a chapel of mischance: ill-luck betide it, 'tis the cursedest kirk that ever I came in!'

Helmet on head and lance in hand, he came up to the rough dwelling, when he heard over the high hill beyond the brook, as it were in a bank, a wondrous fierce noise, that rang in the cliff as if it would cleave asunder. 'Twas as if one ground a scythe on a grindstone, it whirred and whetted like water on a millwheel and rushed and rang, terrible to hear.

'By God,' quoth Gawain, 'I trow that gear is preparing for the knight who will meet me here. Alas! naught may help me, yet should my life be forfeit, I fear not a jot!' With that he called aloud, 'Who waiteth in this place to give me tryst? Now is Gawain come hither: if any man will aught of him let him hasten hither now or never.'

TRANSLATED BY JESSIE WESTON

THE COMING OF THE GREEN KNIGHT

'Stay,' quoth one on the bank above his head, 'and ye shall speedily have that which I promised ye.' Yet for a while the noise of whetting went on ere he appeared, and then he came forth from a cave in the crag with a fell weapon, a Danish axe newly dight, wherewith to deal the blow. An evil head it had, four feet large, no less, sharply ground, and bound to the handle by the lace that gleamed brightly. And the knight himself was all green as before, face and foot, locks and beard, but now he was afoot. When he came to the water he would not wade it, but sprang over with the pole of his axe, and strode boldly over the bent that was white with snow.

Sir Gawain went to meet him, but he made no low bow. The other said, 'Now, fair sir, one may trust thee to keep tryst. Thou art welcome, Gawain, to my place. Thou hast timed thy coming as befits a true man. Thou knowest the covenant set between us: at this time twelve months agone thou didst take that which fell to thee, and I at this New Year will readily requite thee. We are in this valley, verily alone, here are no knights to sever us, do what we will. Have off thy helm from thine head, and have here thy pay; make me no more talking than I did then when thou didst strike off my head with one blow.'

'Nay,' quoth Gawain, 'by God that gave me life, I shall make no moan whatever befall me, but make thou ready for the blow and I shall stand still and say never a word to thee, do as thou wilt.'

With that he bent his head and showed his neck all bare, and made as if he had no fear, for he would not be thought a-dread.

HOW SIR GAWAIN FAILED TO STAND THE BLOW

Then the Green Knight made him ready, and grasped his grim weapon to smite Gawain. With all his force he bore it aloft with a mighty feint of slaying him: had it fallen as straight as he aimed he who was ever doughty of deed had been slain by the blow. But Gawain swerved aside as the axe came gliding down to slay him as he stood, and shrank a little with the shoulders, for the sharp iron. The other heaved up the blade and rebuked the prince with many proud words:

OF THE GREEN KNIGHT'S REPROACHES

'Thou art not Gawain,' he said, 'who is held so valiant, that never feared he man by hill or vale, but *thou* shrinkest for fear ere thou feelest hurt. Such cowardice did *I* never hear of Gawain! Neither did *I* flinch from thy blow, or make strife in King Arthur's hall. My head fell to my feet, and yet I fled not; but thou didst wax faint of heart ere any harm befell. Wherefore must I be deemed the braver knight.'

Quoth Gawain, 'I shrank once, but so will I no more; though an *my* head fall on the stones I cannot replace it. But haste, Sir Knight, by thy faith, and bring me to the point, deal me my destiny, and do it out of hand, for I will stand thee a stroke and move no more till thine axe have hit me – my troth on it.'

'Have at thee, then,' quoth the other, and heaved aloft the axe with fierce mien, as if he were mad. He struck at him fiercely but wounded him not, withholding his hand ere it might strike him.

Gawain abode the stroke, and flinched in no limb, but stood still as a stone or the stump of a tree that is fast rooted in the rocky ground with a hundred roots.

Then spake gaily the man in green, 'So now thou hast thine heart whole it behooves me to smite. Hold aside thy hood that Arthur gave thee, and keep thy neck thus bent lest it cover it again.'

Then Gawain said angrily, 'Why talk on thus? Thou dost threaten too long. I hope thy heart misgives thee.'

HOW THE GREEN KNIGHT DEALT THE BLOW

'For sooth,' quoth the other, 'so fiercely thou speakest I will no longer let thine errand wait its reward.' Then he braced himself to strike, frowning with lips and brow, 'twas no marvel that it pleased but ill him who hoped for no rescue. He lifted the axe lightly and let it fall with the edge of the blade on the bare neck. Though he struck swiftly, it hurt him no more than on the one side where it severed the skin. The sharp blade cut into the flesh so that the blood ran over his shoulder to the ground. And when the knight saw the blood staining the snow, he sprang forth, swift-foot, more than a spear's length, seized his helmet and set it on his head, cast his shield over his shoulder, drew out his bright sword, and spake boldly (never since he was born was he half so blithe), 'Stop, Sir Knight, bid me no more blows. I have stood a stroke here without flinching, and if thou give me another, I shall requite thee, and give thee as good again. By the covenant made betwixt us in Arthur's hall but one blow falls to me here. Halt, therefore.'

OF THE THREE COVENANTS

Then the Green Knight drew off from him and leaned on his axe, setting the shaft on the ground, and looked on Gawain as he stood all armed and faced him fearlessly – at heart it pleased him well. Then he spake merrily in a loud voice, and said to the knight, 'Bold sir, be not so fierce; no man here hath done thee wrong, nor will do, save by covenant, as we made at Arthur's court. I promised thee a blow and thou hast it – hold thyself well paid! I release thee of all other claims. If I had been so minded I might perchance have given thee a rougher buffet. First I menaced thee with a feigned one, and hurt thee not for the covenant that we made in the first night, and which thou didst hold truly. All the gain didst thou give me as a true man should. The other feint I proffered thee for the morrow: my fair wife kissed thee, and thou didst give me her kisses – for both those days I gave thee two blows without scathe – true man, true return. But the third time thou didst fail, and therefore hadst thou that blow. For 'tis my weed thou wearest, that same woven girdle, my own wife wrought it, that do I wot for sooth. Now know I well thy kisses, and thy conversation, and the wooing of my wife, for 'twas mine own doing. I sent her to try thee, and in sooth I think thou art the most faultless knight that ever trod earth. As a pearl among white peas is of more worth than they, so is Gawain, i' faith, by other knights. But thou didst lack a little, Sir Knight, and wast wanting in loyalty, yet that was for no evil work, nor for wooing neither, but because thou lovedst thy life – therefore I blame thee the less.'

THE SHAME OF SIR GAWAIN

Then the other stood a great while, still sorely angered and vexed within himself; all the blood flew to his face, and he shrank for shame as the Green Knight spake; and the first words he said were, 'Cursed be ye, cowardice and covetousness, for in ye is the destruction of virtue.' Then he loosed the girdle, and gave it to the knight. 'Lo, take there the falsity, may foul befall it! For fear of thy blow cowardice bade me make friends with covetousness and forsake the customs of largess and loyalty, which befit all knights. Now am I faulty and false and have been afeared: from treachery and untruth come sorrow and care. I avow to thee, Sir Knight, that I have ill done; do then thy will. I shall be more wary hereafter.'

Then the other laughed and said gaily, 'I wot I am whole of the hurt I had, and thou hast made such free confession of thy misdeeds, and hast so borne the penance of mine axe edge, that I hold thee absolved from that sin, and purged as clean as if thou hadst never sinned since thou wast born. And this girdle that is wrought with gold and green, like my raiment, do I give thee, Sir Gawain, that thou mayest think upon this chance when thou goest forth among princes of renown, and keep this for a token of the adventure of the Green Chapel, as it chanced between chivalrous knights. And thou shalt come again with me to my dwelling and pass the rest of this feast in gladness.' Then the lord laid hold of him, and said, 'I wot we shall soon make peace with my wife, who was thy bitter enemy.'

HOW SIR GAWAIN WOULD KEEP THE GIRDLE

'Nay, forsooth,' said Sir Gawain, and seized his helmet and took it off swiftly, and thanked the knight: 'I have fared ill, may bliss betide thee, and may He who rules all things reward thee swiftly. Commend me to that courteous lady, thy fair wife, and to the other my honoured ladies, who have beguiled their knight with skilful craft. But 'tis no marvel if one be made a fool and brought to sorrow by women's wiles, for so was Adam beguiled by one, and Solomon by many, and Samson all too soon, for Delilah dealt him his doom; and David thereafter was wedded with Bathsheba, which brought him much sorrow – if one might love a woman and believe her not, 'twere great gain! And since all they were beguiled by women, methinks 'tis the less blame to me that I was misled! But as for thy girdle, that will I take with good will, not for gain of the gold, nor for samite, nor silk, nor the costly pendants, neither for weal nor for worship, but in sign of my frailty. I shall look upon it when I ride in renown and remind myself of the fault and faintness of the flesh; and so when pride uplifts me for prowess of arms, the sight of this lace shall humble my heart. But one thing would I pray, if it displease thee not: since thou art lord of yonder land wherein I have dwelt, tell me what thy rightful name may be and I will ask no more.'

HOW THE MARVEL WAS WROUGHT

'That will I truly,' quoth the other. 'Bernlak de Hautdesert am I called in this land. Morgain le Fay dwelleth in mine house, and through knowledge of clerkly craft hath she taken many. For long time was she the mistress of Merlin, who knew well all you knights of the court. Morgain the goddess is she called therefore, and there is none so haughty but she can bring him low. She sent me in this guise to yon fair hall to test the truth of the renown that is spread abroad of the valour of the Round Table. She taught me this marvel to betray your wits, to vex Guinevere and fright her to death by the man who spake with his head in his hand at the high table. That is she who is at home, that ancient lady, she is even thine aunt, Arthur's half-sister, the daughter of the Duchess of Tintagel, who afterward married King Uther. Therefore I bid thee, knight, come to thine aunt, and make merry in thine house; my folk love thee, and I wish thee as well as any man on earth, by my faith, for thy true dealing.'

But Sir Gawain said nay, he would in no wise do so; so they embraced and kissed, and commended each other to the Prince of Paradise, and parted right there, on the cold ground. Gawain on his steed rode swiftly to the king's hall, and the Green Knight got him whithersoever he would.

HOW SIR GAWAIN CAME AGAIN TO CAMELOT

Sir Gawain, who had thus won grace of his life, rode through wild ways on Gringalet; oft he lodged in a house, and oft without, and many adventures did he have and came off victor full often, as at this time I cannot relate in tale. The hurt that he had in his neck was healed, he bare the shining girdle as a baldric bound by his side, and made fast with a knot 'neath his left arm, in token that he was taken in a fault – and thus he came in safety again to the court.

Then joy awakened in that dwelling when the king knew that the good Sir Gawain was come, for he deemed it gain. King Arthur kissed the knight, and the queen also, and many valiant knights sought to embrace him. They asked him how he had fared, and he told them all that had chanced to him – the adventure of the chapel, the fashion of the knight, the love of the lady – at last of the lace. He showed them the wound in the neck which he won for his disloyalty at the hand of the knight; the blood flew to his face for shame as he told the tale.

SIR GAWAIN MAKES CONFESSION OF HIS FAULT
'Lo, lady,' he quoth, and handled the lace, 'this is the bond of the blame that I bear in my neck, this is the harm and the loss I have suffered, the cowardice and covetousness in which I was caught, the token of my covenant in which I was taken. And I must needs wear it so long as I live, for none may hide his harm, but undone it may not be, for if it hath clung to thee once, it may never be severed.'

THE KNIGHTS WEAR THE LACE IN HONOUR OF GAWAIN
Then the king comforted the knight, and the court laughed loudly at the tale, and all made accord that the lords and the ladies who belonged to the Round Table, each hero among them, should wear bound about him a bawdrick of bright green for the sake of Sir Gawain.

THE END OF THE TALE
And to this was agreed all the honour of the Round Table, and he who ware it was honoured the more thereafter, as it is testified in the best book of romance. That in Arthur's days this adventure befell, the book of Brutus bears witness. For since that bold knight came hither first, and the siege and the assault were ceased at Troy, I wis

> Many a venture herebeforn
> Hath fallen such as this:
> May He that bare the crown of thorn
> Bring us unto His bliss.

Amen.

Book I

I

Since Troy's assault and siege, I trow, were over-past,
To brands and ashes burnt that stately burg at last,
And he, the traitor proved, for treason that he
    wrought,
Was fitly tried and judged, – his fortune elsewhere
    sought
The truest knight on earth, Æneas, with his kin,
Who vanquished provinces, and did, as princes, win
Of all the Western Isles, the wealth and worth alway;
Rich Romulus to Rome full swift hath ta'en his way,
First, hath he founded fair that city in his pride
To which he gave his name, it bears it to this tide;
Ticius doth dwellings found, turning to Tuscany,
And Langobard, a race raised up in, Lombardy.
But Felix Brutus sailed full far, o'er the French flood,
And on its banks so broad founded Britain, the good,
    in bliss;
    Where war nor wonder fail
    And ne'er have done, ywis,
    Nor shall both bliss and bale
    their shifting chances miss.

TRANSLATED BY JESSIE WESTON

II

And when that baron bold had Britain made, I trow,
Bold men were bred therein, who loved strife well
  enow,
And many a war they waged in those good days of
  yore—
Of marvels stern and strange, in this land many more
Have chanced than otherwhere, since that same time,
  I ween—
But of all kings who e'er o'er Britain lords have been,
Fairest was Arthur all, and boldest, so men tell;
Therefore I think to shew a venture that befell
In his time, which some men for a sheer wonder hold,
And strange above all tales that be of Arthur told.
If ye will list this lay a little while, in sooth,
I'll tell ye as I heard it told in town for truth
    with tongue—
    As it doth stand, to wit,
    In story stiff and strong,
    In letters fairly writ,
    The land hath known it long.

III

At Camelot lay the King, all on a Christmas-tide,
With many a lovely lord, and gallant knight beside,
And of the Table Round did the rich brotherhood
High revel hold aright, and mirthful was their mood:
Oft-times on tourney bent those gallants sought the
  field,
And gentle knights in joust would shiver spear and
  shield;
Anon would seek the court for sport and carol gay—

For fifteen days full told the feast was held alway,
With all the meat and mirth that men might well devise,
Right glorious was the glee that rang in riotous wise.
Glad clamour through the day, dancing throughout the night;
Good luck throughout the hall and chambers well bedight,
Had lords and ladies fair, each one as pleased him best,
With all of this world's weal they dwelt, those gallant guests;
For Christ no braver knights had faced or toil or strife,
No fairer ladies e'er had drawn the breath of life,
And he, the comeliest king that e'er held court, forsooth,
For all this goodly folk were e'en in their first youth,
and still
    The happiest under heaven,
    A king of stalwart will,
    'T were hard with them to even
    Another host on hill!

IV

So young the New Year was, methinks it just was born,
Double upon the dais they served the meat that morn;
Into the hall he came, with all his knights, the King,
E'en as the chapel choir to end the mass did sing.
Loud rang the voice of clerk and cantor there aloft,
'*Nowell, Nowell!*' they sang, and cried the word full oft.
And sithen forth they run for handsel fair and free

Their New Year's gifts they pray, or give them readily.
And then about the gifts they make debate enow,
And ladies laugh full loud, tho' they have lost, I trow!
And this I rede ye well, not wroth was he who won!—
And all this mirth they made till meal-time came – anon
The board was set, they washed, and then in order meet
The noblest aye above, each gallant took his seat.
When Gaynore, gayly clad, stepped forth among them all,
Upon the royal dais, high in the midmost hall.
Sendal swept at her side, and eke above her head
A tapestry of Tars, and choice Toulouse outspread,
And all embroidered fair, and set with gems so gay
That might be proved of price, an ye their worth would pay
    one day;
      Right fair she was, the queen,
      With eyes of shining grey,
      That fairer he had seen
      No man might soothly say!

V

Arthur, he would not eat till all were served with food,
Glad of his gladness he, somewhat of child-like mood;
A changeful life he loved, he liked it not a whit,
Either o'er-long to lie, or e'en o'er-long to sit,
So chafed his youthful blood, and eke his busy brain.
Also a custom good, to which the King was fain—
Thro' valour 'stablished fast – that never would he eat
On such high holiday ere yet adventure meet

SIR GAWAIN AND THE GREEN KNIGHT

Were told unto his ear – or wondrous tale enow,
Or else some marvel great that he might well allow—
Tales of his father's days, of arms, of emprise high,—
Or e'en some knight besought another's skill to try,
To join with him in joust, in jeopardy to lay
Life against life, each one, on hap of knightly play.
As Fortune them might aid – in quest of honour fair—
This was his custom good when as in court he were
At each high holiday, among his courtiers there
   in hall,
      Fair-faced, and free of fear,
      He sitteth o'er them all,
      Right keen in that New Year,
      And maketh mirth withal.

VI

Thus in his place he stands, the young and gallant king,
Before the royal board, talking of many a thing.
There good Gawain, gay clad, beside Gaynore doth sit,
Agravain '*dure main*,' beyond her as is fit;
(Both the King's sister's sons, and knights of valiant mood—)
High at the table sits Baldwin the Bishop good,
And Ywain, Urien's son, doth with the Bishop eat—
These on the daïs are served, in seemly wise, and meet.
Full many a gallant knight sits at the board below;
See where the first course comes, while loud the trumpets blow!
With many a banner bright that gaily waves thereby,
And royal roll of drums, and pipes that shrill on high.

Wild warblings waken there, and sweet notes rise and fall,
Till many a heart swelled high within that castle hall!
Dainties they bring therewith, and meats both choice and rare—
Such plenty of fresh food, so many dishes bear,
They scarce might find a place to set, the folk before,
The silver vessels all that savoury messes bore,
  on cloth,
    The guests they help themselves,
    Thereto they be not loth,
    Each twain had dishes twelve,
    Good beer, and red wine both.

VII

Now of their service good I think no more to say,
For each man well may wot no lack was there that day.
Noise that to them was new methinks now drew anear
Such as each man in hall were ever fain to hear,
For scarce the joyful sounds unto an end were brought,
And scarce had the first course been fitly served at court,
When through the hall door rushed a champion, fierce and fell,
Highest in stature he, of all on earth who dwell!
From neck to waist so square, and eke so thickly set,
His loins and limbs alike, so long they were, and great,
Half giant upon earth, I hold him to have been,
In every way of men the tallest he, I ween—
The merriest in his might that e'er a joust might ride,
Sternly his body framed in back, and breast, and side,

Belly and waist alike were fitly formed, and small,
E'en so his features fair were sharply cut withal,
   and clean,
     Men marvelled at his hue,
     So was his semblance seen,
     He fared as one on feud,
     And overall was green!

VIII

All green bedight that knight, and green his garments fair
A narrow coat that clung straight to his side he ware,
A mantle plain above, lined on the inner side
With costly fur and fair, set on good cloth and wide,
So sleek, and bright in hue – therewith his hood was gay
Which from his head was doffed, and on his shoulders lay.
Full tightly drawn his hose, all of the self-same green,
Well clasped about his calf – there-under spurs full keen
Of gold on silken lace, all striped in fashion bright,
That dangled beneath his legs – so rode that gallant knight.
His vesture, verily, was green as grass doth grow,
The barring of his belt, the blithe stones set arow,
That decked in richest wise his raiment fine and fair,
Himself, his saddle-bow, in silken broideries rare,
'T were hard to tell the half, so cunning was the wise
In which 't was broidered all with birds, and eke with flies!
Decked was the horse's neck, and decked the crupper bold,

With gauds so gay of green, the centre set with gold.
And every harness boss was all enamelled green,
The stirrups where he stood were of the self same sheen,
The saddle-bow behind, the girths so long and fair,
They gleamed and glittered all with green stones rich and rare,
The very steed beneath the self same semblance ware, he rides
    A green horse great and tall;
    A steed full stiff to guide,
    In broidered bridle all
    He worthily bestrides!

IX

Right gaily was the knight bedecked, all green his weed,
The hair upon his head, the mane of his good steed,
Fair floating locks enfold his shoulders broad and strong,
Great as a bush the beard that on his breast low hung,
And, with his goodly hair that hung down from his head,
A covering round his arms, above his elbows, spread.
Laced were his arms below, e'en in the self-same way
As a king's cap-a dos, that clasps his neck alway.
The mane of that great steed was well and deftly wrought,
Well crisped and combed the hair, with many a knot in-caught.
Folded with golden thread about the green so fair,
Here lay a twist of gold, and here a coil of hair.

In self-same wise the tail and top-most crest were
   twined,
A band of brightest green the twain alike did bind,
Which, set with precious stones, hung the tail's length
   adown,
Then, twisted in a knot, on high the crest did crown.
There-from hung many a bell, of burnished gold so
   bright.,
Such foal upon the fell, bestridden by such knight,
Sure ne'er within that hall before of mortal sight
   were seen,
>   As lightning gleaming bright
>   So seemed to all his sheen,
>   They deemed that no man might
>   Endure his blows so keen.

X

Nor helmet on his head, nor hauberk did he wear,
Gorget nor breast-plate good, as knights are wont to
   bear;
Nor shaft to smite, nor shield that blows might well
   withstand,
Naught but a holly bough he carried in one hand,
(When all the groves be bare then fullest is its green),
And in his other hand a huge axe, sharp and sheen,
A weapon ill to see, would one its fashion say,
The haft, it measured full an ell-yard long alway,
The blade of good green steel, and all with gold inlaid,
Right sharp and broad the edge, and burnished bright
   the blade.
'T was sharpened well to cut, e'en as a razor good,
Right well the steel was set in staff so stiff of wood,
And iron bands to bind throughout the length it bare,

With cunning work of green all wrought, and graven
    fair.
Twined with a lace that fell in silken loops so soft
E'en at the head, adown the haft 't was caught full oft
With hanging tassells fair that silken threads entwine,
And buttons of bright green, all broidered fair and
    fine.
Thus in the great hall door the knight stood, fair and
    tall,
Fearless and free his gaze, he gat him down the hall,
Greeting he gave to none, but looked right steadily
Toward the royal seat, and quoth, 'Now where is he,
The lord of all this folk? To see him am I fain,
And with himself would speak, might I the boon
    attain!'—
   With frown
      He looked upon the knights,
      And paced him up and down,
      Fain would he know aright
      Who was of most renown!

XI

Then each man gazed amain, each would that hero
    see,
And each man marvelled much what might the
    meaning be,
That man and horse, alike, of such a hue were seen,
Green as the growing grass; and greener still, I ween,
E'en than enamel green on gold that gloweth bright:
Then all with one consent drew near unto that knight,
A-marvelling fell they all who he might be, ywis,
For strange sights had they seen, but none so strange
    as this!

The folk, they deemed it well fantasm, or faërie,
And none among them all dare answer speedily,
But all, astonied, gazed, and held them still as stone,
Throughout that goodly hall, in silence every one,
Their faces changed, as they by sleep were overcome,
   suddenly,
      I deem not all for fear,
      But some for courtesy,
      They fain would lend an ear
      And let the King reply.

XII

Arthur before his daïs beheld this marvel fair,
And boldly did he speak for dread, he knew it ne'er—
And said: Right welcome, Sir, to this my house and
   hall,
Head of this hostel I, and *Arthur*, men me call.
Alight from this thy steed, and linger here, I pray,
And what thy will may be hereafter shalt thou say.'
'So help me,' quoth the knight, 'the God who rules
   o'er all,
I came not here to bide within thy castle wall,
The praise of this thy folk throughout the world is
   told,
Thy burg, thy barons all, bravest and best they hold,
The stiffest under steel who battle-steed bestride,
Wisest and worthiest they, throughout the whole
   world wide,
Proven right well in joust, and all fair knightly play,
Renowned for courtesy – so have I heard men say—
And this hath brought me here, e'en at this Yule-tide
   fair,
For be ye well assured by this green branch I bear

TRANSLATED BY JESSIE WESTON

That I would pass in peace, and seek no battle here—
For an it were my will to ride in warlike gear
I have at home an helm, and hauberk good and strong,
A shield and shining spear, with blade both sharp and long,
And other weapons good, that well a knight beseem,
But since I seek no war my weeds are soft, I ween,
And if ye be so bold as all men say ye be
The favour that I ask ye sure will grant to me
   of right,'
     Arthur, he was not slow
     To speak, 'I trow, Sir Knight,
     An here thou seek'st a foe
     Thou shalt not fail for fight!'

XIII

'Nay, here I crave no fight, in sooth I say to thee,
The knights about thy board but beardless bairns they be,
An I were fitly armed, upon this steed so tall,
For lack of strength no man might match me in this hall!
Therefore within thy court I crave a Christmas jest,
'T is Yuletide, and New Year, and here be many a guest,
If any in this hall himself so hardy hold,
So valiant of his hand, of blood and brain so bold,
That stroke for counter-stroke with me exchange he dare,
I give him of free gift this gisarme rich and fair,
This axe of goodly weight, to wield as he see fit,
And I will bide his blow, as bare as here I sit.
If one will test my words, and be of valiant mood,

SIR GAWAIN AND THE GREEN KNIGHT

Then let him swiftly come, and take this weapon good,—
Here I renounce my claim, the axe shall be his own—
And I will stand his stroke, here, on this floor of stone,
That I in turn a blow may deal, that boon alone
   I pray,
     Yet respite shall he have
     A twelvemonth, and a day.
     Now quickly I thee crave—
     Who now hath aught to say?'

XIV

If erst they were amazed, now stiller sat they all,
Both high and low, those knights within King Arthur's hall,
The knight upon his steed he sat him fast and true,
And round about the hall his fierce red eyes he threw,
From 'neath his bushy brows, (all green they were in hue,)
Twisting his beard he waits to see if none will rise,
When no man proffers speech with mocking voice he cries,
'What, is this Arthur's house? Is this his gallant band
Whose fame hath run abroad through many a realm and land?
Where be your vaunted pride? Your conquests, where be they?
Your wrath, and fierceness fell, your boastful words alway?
Now is the Table Round, its revel and renown,
O'erthrown with but a word from one man's mouth alone,
Since none dare speak for dread tho' ne'er a dint he see.—'

With that he laughed so loud Arthur must shaméd be,
And in his face so fair the blood rose ruddily
   alight,
      As wind waxed wroth the King
      And every gallant knight,
      In words of warlike ring
      He hailed that man of might.

XV

And quoth, 'By Heaven, Sir Knight, thou speakest
   foolishly,
But what thy folly craves we needs must grant to thee,
I trow no knight of mine thy boastful words doth fear,
That goodly axe of thine in God's name give me here,
And I will give the boon which thou dost here
   demand!'
With that he lightly leapt, and caught him by the
   hand,
Then lighted down the knight, before the King he
   stood,
And Arthur, by the haft he gripped that axe so good,
And swung it sternly round, as one who thought to
   smite;
Before him on the floor he stood, that stranger knight,
Taller by full a head than any in the hall,
With stern mien did he stand, and stroked his beard
   withal,
And drew his coat adown, e'en with unruffled cheer,
No more was he dismayed for threats he needs must
   hear
Than at the royal board one bare a cup anear
   of wine,
      Gawain from out his place

Spake fitting words and fine,
'I pray thee of thy grace
Be this adventure mine!'

XVI

Quoth Gawain to the King, 'I pray right worthily
Thou bid me quit this seat, and take my stand by thee,
That so without reproach, I from this board may rise,
And that it be not ill in my liege lady's eyes,
I'll to thy counsel come before this royal court,
Unfitting do I deem that such a boon be sought,
And such a challenge raised in this your goodly hall
That thou thyself be fain to answer it withal,
While many a valiant knight doth sit beside thee still—
I wot there be 'neath Heaven no men of sterner will,
Nor braver on the field where men fight as is fit—
Methinks, the weakest I, the feeblest here of wit,
The less loss of my life, if thou the sooth would'st say!
Save as thy near of kin no praise were mine alway,
No virtue save thy blood I in my body know!
Since this be folly all, nor thine to strike this blow,
And I have prayed the boon, then grant it unto me,
This good court, an I bear myself ungallantly,
    may blame!'
        Together did they press,
        Their counsel was the same,
        To free the King, no less,
        And give Gawain the game.

TRANSLATED BY JESSIE WESTON

XVII

Then did the King command that gallant knight to rise,
And swiftly up he gat in fair and courteous wise,
And knelt before his lord, and gripped the axe's haft,
The King, he loosed his hold, and raised his hand aloft,
And blessed him in Christ's Name, and bade him in good part
To be of courage still, hardy of hand and heart.
'Now, Nephew, keep thee well,' he quoth, 'deal but one blow,
And if thou red'st him well, in very truth I know
The blow that he shall deal thou shalt right well withstand!'
Gawain strode to the knight, the gisarme in his hand,
Right boldly did he bide, no whit abashed, I ween,
And frankly to Gawain he quoth, that knight in green,
'Make we a covenant here, ere yet we further go,
And first I ask, Sir Knight, that I thy name may know,
I bid thee tell me true, that I assured may be—'
'I' faith,' quoth that good knight, '*Gawain*, I wot, is he
Who giveth thee this blow, be it for good or ill,
A twelvemonth hence I'll take another at thy will,
The weapon be thy choice, I'll crave no other still alive!'
    The other quoth again,
    'Gawain, so may I thrive,
    But I shall take full fain,
    The dint that thou shalt drive!'

XVIII

'By Christ,' quoth the Green Knight, 'I trow I am full fain
The blow that here I craved to take from thee, Gawain,
And thou hast well rehearsed, in fashion fair, I trow,
The covenant and the boon I prayed the king but now;
Save that thou here, Sir Knight, shalt soothly swear to me
To seek me out thyself, where e'er it seemeth thee
I may be found on field, and there in turn demand
Such dole as thou shalt deal before this goodly band!'
'Now,' quoth the good Gawain, 'by Him who fashioned me,
I wot not where to seek, nor where thy home shall be,
I know thee not, Sir Knight, thy court, nor yet thy name,
Teach me thereof the truth, and tell me of that same,
And I will use my wit to win me to that goal,
And here I give thee troth, and swear it on my soul!'
'Nay, in this New Year's tide it needs no more, I ween,'
So to the good Gawain he quoth, that knight in green,
'Save that I tell thee true – when I the blow have ta'en,
Which thou shalt smartly smite – and teach thee here amain
Where be my house, my home, and what my name shall be;
Then may'st thou find thy road, and keep thy pledge with me.
But if I waste no speech, thou shalt the better speed,
And in thy land may'st dwell, nor further seek at need for fight

Take thy grim tool to thee,
Let see how thou can'st smite!'
Quoth Gawain, 'Willingly,'
And stroked his axe so bright.

XIX

The Green Knight on the ground made ready speedily,
He bent his head adown, that so his neck were free,
His long and lovely locks, across the crown they fell,
His bare neck to the nape all men might see right well
Gawain, he gripped his axe, and swung it up on high,
The left foot on the ground he setteth steadily
Upon the neck so bare he let the blade alight,
The sharp edge of the axe the bones asunder smite—
Sheer thro' the flesh it smote, the neck was cleft in two,
The brown steel on the ground it bit, so strong the blow,
The fair head from the neck fell even to the ground,
Spurned by the horse's hoof, e'en as it rolled around,
The red blood spurted forth, and stained the green so bright,
But ne'er for that he failed, nor fell, that stranger knight,
Swiftly he started up, on stiff and steady limb,
And stretching forth his hand, as all men gaped at him,
Grasped at his goodly head, and lift it up again,
Then turned him to his steed, and caught the bridle rein,
Set foot in stirrup-iron, bestrode the saddle fair,
The while he gripped his head e'en by the flowing hair.

He set himself as firm in saddle, so I ween,
As naught had ailed him there, tho' headless he was
    seen
  in hall;
    He turned his steed about,
    That corpse, that bled withal,
    Full many there had doubt
    Of how the pledge might fall!

XX

The head, within his hand he held it up a space,
Toward the royal dais, forsooth, he turned the face,
The eyelids straight were raised, and looked with
    glance so clear,
Aloud it spake, the mouth, e'en as ye now may hear;
'Look, Gawain, thou be swift to speed as thou hast
    said,
And seek, in all good faith, until thy search be sped,
E'en as thou here didst swear, in hearing of these
    knights—
To the Green Chapel come, I charge thee now aright,
The blow thou hast deserved, such as was dealt to-day,
E'en on the New Year's morn I pledge me to repay,
Full many know my name, "*Knight of the Chapel
    Green*,"
To find me, should'st thou seek, thou wilt not fail, I
    ween,
Therefore thou need'st must come, or be for recreant
    found!'
With fierce pull at the rein he turned his steed
    around,
His head within his hand, forth from the hall he rode,
Beneath his horse's hoofs the sparks they flew abroad,

No man in all the hall wist where he took his way,
Nor whence that knight had come durst any of them
   say,
   what then?
      The King and Gawain there
      They gazed, and laughed again,
      Proven it was full fair
      A marvel unto men!

XXI

Tho' Arthur in his heart might marvel much, I ween,
No semblance in his speech of fear or dread was seen
Unto the Queen he quoth, in courteous wise, and gay,
'Dear lady, at this tide let naught your heart dismay,
Such craft doth well, methinks, to Christmas-time
   belong,
When jests be soothly sought, with laugh and merry
   song,
And when in carols gay our knights and ladies vie—
Natheless unto my meat I'll get me presently,
I may not soon forget the sight mine eyes have seen!'
He turned him to Gawain, and quoth with gladsome
   mien,
'Now, Sir, hang up thine axe, the blow was soundly
   sped!'
'T was hung above the dais, on dossel overhead,
That all within the hall might look upon it well,
And by that token true the tale of wonder tell,
Then to the royal board they sat them down, those
   twain,
The King, and the good knight, and men for service
   fain
As to the noblest there with double portion wend—

With meat and minstrelsy the Yule-tide feast they
   spend,
With joy they pass the day till shades of night descend
   o'er land,
    Now think thee well, Gawain,
    And fail not to withstand
    The venture thou wast fain
    To take unto thine hand!

Book II

I

Now this first venture fair, befell in the New Year
To Arthur, who such feats was ever fain to hear;
Altho' his words were few whenas at meat they met;
But now to task full stern their hand methinks be set.
Right gladly did Gawain begin these games in hall,
If heavy be the end, small wonder were withal:
A man hath merry mind when he hath drunk amain,
Speedy, the year hath sped and cometh not again;
Beginnings to their end do all unlike appear—
The Yuletide passed away; and eke the after year
Each season severally after the other sent;
When Christmas-tide was past then came the crabbéd Lent,
That, changing flesh for fish, doth simpler food provide;
The weather of the world with winter then doth chide,
The cold no longer clings, the clouds themselves uplift,

Shed swift the rain, and warm, the showers of
  springtide drift,
Fall fair upon the field, the flowers all unfold,
The grass, and e'en the groves all green ye may
  behold.
The birds begin to build, and greet, with joyful song,
Solace of summer sweet, that followeth ere long—
  On bank
    The blossoms fair they blow
    In hedgerow rich and rank;
    The birds sing loud and low
    In woodland deep and dank.

II

After the summer-tide, with gentle winds and soft,
When zephyr on the sward and seeds doth breathe full
  oft,
(Full gladsome is the growth waxing therefrom, I
  ween,
Whenas the dewdrops drip from off the leaves so
  green,
Beneath the blissful beams of the bright summer
  sun)—
Then nigheth harvest-tide, hardening the grain anon,
With warnings to wax ripe ere come the winter cold,
With drought he drives the dust before him on the
  wold,
From off the field it flies, in clouds it riseth high;
Winds of the welkin strive with the sun, wrathfully,
The leaves fall from the bough, and lie upon the
  ground,
And grey is now the grass that erst all green was
  found;

Ripens and rots the fruit that once was flower gay—
And thus the year doth turn to many a yesterday,
Winter be come again, as needeth not to say
    the sage;
        Then, when Saint Michael's moon
        Be come with winter's gage
        Gawain bethinks him soon
        Of his dread venture's wage.

III

Yet till All-Hallows' Day with Arthur did he bide,
Then for his sake the king a fair feast did provide,
Rich was the revel there of the good Table Round,
There were both courteous knights and comely ladies
    found,
And many sorrowed sore all for that good knight's
    sake—
Yet none the less no sign of aught but mirth they
    make,
Tho' joyless all the jests they bandy at that same—
With mourning after meat he to his uncle came,
And of his journey spake, and openly did say:
'Now, liege Lord of my life, your leave I fain would
    pray,
Ye know how stands the case, thereof no more I'll
    speak—
Since talk, it mendeth naught, 't were trifling ease to
    seek;
I to the blow am bound, to-morrow must I fare
To seek the Knight in Green, God knoweth how, or
    where.'
The best knights in the burg together then they ran,
Ywain and Erec there, with many another man,

Dodinel le Sauvage; the Duke of Clarence came,
Lancelot, Lionel, and Lucain, at that same,
Sir Boors, Sir Bedivere, (the twain were men of might,)
With Mador de la Port, and many another knight.
Courtiers in company nigh to the king they drew,
For counselling that knight, much care at heart they knew.
In dole so drear their tears in hall together blend
To think that good Gawain must on such errand wend
Such dolefull dint endure, no more fair blows to spend and free—
    The knight he made good cheer,
    He quoth: 'What boots it me?
    For tho' his weird be drear
    Each man that same must dree.'

IV

He dwelt there all that day, at early dawn besought
That men would bring his arms, and all were straightway brought.
A carpet on the floor they stretch full fair and tight,
Rich was the golden gear that on it glittered bright.
The brave man stepped thereon, the steel he handled fair,
A doublet dear of Tars they did upon him there,
A cunning cap-a-dos, that fitted close and well,
All fairly lined throughout, as I have heard it tell.
They set the shoes of steel upon the hero's feet,
And wrapped the legs in greaves, of steel, as fit and meet.
The caps that 'longed thereto polished they were full clean,

And knit about the knee with knots of golden sheen.
Comely the cuisses were that closed him all about
With thongs all tightly tied around his thighs so stout.
And then a byrnie bright with burnished steel they
    bring,
Upon a stuff so fair woven with many a ring.
And now upon each arm they set the burnished brace
With elbow plates so good – the metal gloves they
    lace;
Thus all the goodly gear to shield him was in place
    that tide—
        Rich surcoat doth he wear,
        And golden spurs of pride,
        His sword is girt full fair
        With silk, upon his side.

V

When he was fitly armed his harness rich they deem,
Nor loop nor latchet small but was with gold a-gleam;
Then, harnessed as he was, his Mass he heard
    straightway,
On the high altar there an offering meet did lay.
Then, coming to the king, and to the knights at court,
From lords and ladies fair lightly his leave besought.
They kissed the knight, his soul commending to
    Christ's care—
Ready was Gringalet, girt with a saddle fair,
Gaily it gleamed that day, with fringes all of gold,
For this adventure high new nails it bare for old.
The bridle barred about, with gold adornéd well,
The harness of the neck, the skirts that proudly fell,
Crupper and coverture match with the saddle-bow,
On all the red gold nails were richly set a-row,

They glittered and they gleamed, e'en as the sun, I wis—
The knight, he takes his helm, and greets it with a kiss.
'T was hooped about with steel, and all full fitly lined,
He set it on his head, and hasped it close behind.
Over the visor, lo! a kerchief lieth light,
Broidered about and bound with goodly gems and bright,
On a broad silken braid – there many a bird is seen
The painted perroquet appeareth there between
Turtles and true-love knots, so thick entwinéd there,
As maids seven winters long had wrought with labour fair
in town;
    Full dear the circlet's price
    That lay around the crown,
    Of diamonds its device
    That were both bright and brown.

VI

The shield they shewed him then, of flaming gules so red,
There the Pentangle shines, in pure gold burnishéd.
On baldric bound, the shield, he to his neck makes tight,
Full well I ween, that sign became the comely knight;
And why unto that prince the badge doth well pertain,
Tarry thereby my tale, I yet to tell am fain.
(For Solomon as sign erst the Pentangle set
In tokening of truth, it bears that title yet.)
For 't is in figure formed of full five points I ween,
Each line in other laced, no ending there is seen.

Each doth the other lock – in English land, I wot,
It beareth everywhere the name of 'Endless Knot.'
Therefore as fitting badge the knight this sign doth wear,
For faithful he in five, five-fold the gifts he bare,
Sir Gawain, good was he, pure as refinéd gold,
Void of all villainy, virtue did him enfold,
    and grace—
        So the Pentangle new
        Hath on his shield a place,
        As knight of heart most true,
        Fairest of form and face.

VII

First was he faultless found in his five wits, I ween;
Nor failed his fingers five where'er he yet had been;
And all his earthly trust upon those five wounds lay
That Christ won on the Cross, e'en as the Creed doth say.
And wheresoever Fate to fiercest fight did bring,
Truly in thought he deemed, above all other thing,
That all his force, forsooth, from those five joys he drew
Which through her Holy Child, the Queen of Heaven knew;
And for this cause the knight, courteous and comely, bare
On one half of his shield her image painted fair,
That when he looked thereon his courage might not fail
The fifth five that I find did much this knight avail
Were Frankness, Fellowship, all other gifts above,
Cleanness and Courtesy, that ever did him move,

And Pity, passing all – I trow in this fair five
That knight was clothed and happed o'er all that be alive.
And all these gifts, fivefold, upon that knight were bound,
Each in the other linked, that none an end had found.
Fast fixed upon five points, I trow, that failed him ne'er,
Nor joined at any side, nor sundered anywhere.
Nor was there any point, so cunningly they blend,
Where they beginning make, or where they find an end.
Therefore, upon his shield, fair-shapen, doth that same
Sign, in fair red gold gleam, upon red gules aflame,
Which the Pentangle pure the folk do truly name
with lore
    Armed is Sir Gawain gay,
    His lance aloft he bore,
    And wished them all 'Good-day,'
    He deemed, for evermore.

VIII

Spurs to his steed he set, and sprang upon his way,
So that from out the stones the sparks they flew alway—
Seeing that seemly sight the hearts of all did sink,
Each soothly said to each that which they secret think,
Grieved for that comely knight – 'By Christ, 't were pity great
If yon good knight be lost, who is of fair estate;
His peer on field to find, i' faith, it were not light,
'T were better to have wrought by wile, methinks, than might!

Such doughty knight a duke were worthier to have
   been,
A leader upon land, gladly we such had seen!—
Such lot were better far than he were brought to
   naught,
Hewn by an elfish man, for gage of prideful thought!
Did ever any king obey such strange behest,
As risk a goodly knight upon a Christmas jest?'
Much water warm, I ween, welled from the eyes of all,
Whenas that gallant knight gat him from Arthur's hall
   that day:
   Nor here would he abide,
   But swiftly went his way,
   By toilsome paths did ride,
   E'en as the book doth say.

IX

Now rides Gawain the good thro' Logres' realm, I
   trow,
Forth doth he fare on quest that seemeth ill enow;
Often, companionless, at night alone must lie,
The fare he liketh best he lacketh verily;
No fellow save his foal hath he by wood or wold,
With none save God alone that knight may converse
   hold;
Till that unto North Wales full nigh he needs must
   draw,
The isles of Anglesey on his left hand he saw;
And fared across the ford and foreland at that same,
Over 'gainst Holyhead, so that he further came
To Wirral's wilds, methinks, nor long therein abode
Since few within that land, they love or man, or God!
And ever as he fared he asked the folk, I ween,

TRANSLATED BY JESSIE WESTON

If they had heard men tell tale of a Knight in Green
In all that land about? Or of a Chapel Green?
And all men answered, 'Nay,' naught of that knight they knew,
And none had seen with sight a man who bare such hue
  as green;
 The knight took roads full strange,
 And rugged paths between,
 His mood full oft did change
 Ere he his goal had seen.

X

Full many a cliff he climbs within that country's range,
Far flying from his friends he rideth lone and strange;
At every ford and flood he passed upon his way
He found a foe before, of fashion grim alway.
So foul they were, and fell, that he of needs must fight—
So many a marvel there befell that gallant knight
That tedious 't were to tell the tithe thereof, I ween
Sometimes with worms he warred, or wolves his foes have been;
Anon with woodmen wild, who in the rocks do hide—
Of bulls, or bears, or boars, the onslaught doth he bide;
And giants, who drew anigh, from off the moorland height;
Doughty in durance he, and shielded by God's might
Else, doubtless, had he died, full oft had he been slain.
Yet war, it vexed him less than winter's bitter bane,

When the clear water cold from out the clouds was
    shed,
And froze ere yet it fell on fallow field and dead;
Then, more nights than enow, on naked rocks he lay,
And, half slain with the sleet, in harness slept alway.
While the cold spring that erst its waters clattering
    flung
From the cliff high o'erhead, in icicles now hung.
In peril thus, and pain, and many a piteous plight
Until the Yuletide Eve alone that gallant knight
        did fare;
    Sir Gawain, at that tide,
    To Mary made his prayer,
    For fain he was to ride
    Where he might shelter share.

XI

That morn beside a mount his road the knight doth
    keep,
Threading a forest wild, with ways both strange and
    deep;
High hills on either hand, and holts full thick below,
Where hoar oaks, hundredfold, do close together grow;
Hazel and hawthorn there, in tangled thicket clung,
Ragged and rough, the moss o'er all a covering flung.
And many birds unblithe, on boughs ye might behold,
Piping full piteously, for pain of bitter cold.
Gawain, on Gringalet, fares lonely thro' the glade,
Thro' many a miry marsh, at heart full sore afraid
That he no shelter find, that, as was fit and right
He serve betimes that Sire, who, on that selfsame
    night
Was of a Maiden born, our bale to cure, I trow—

Therefore he, sighing, said: 'Lord Christ, I pray Thee now,
And Mary Mother mild, for her Son's sake so dear,
A haven I may find, Thy mass may fitly hear,
And matins at the morn – meekly I crave this boon,
And Paternoster pray, and Ave too, right soon,
  with Creed—'
    Thus praying, did he ride,
    Confessing his misdeed,
    Crossing himself, he cried:
    'Christ's Cross me better speed!'

XII

Scarce had he signed himself, I ween, of times but three,
When there within the wood a dwelling doth he see;
Above a laund, on lawe, shaded by many a bough,
About its moat there stand of stately trees enow.
The comeliest castle sure, for owner strong and stout,
Set in a meadow fair with park all round about,
Within a palisade of spikes set thick and close,
For more than two miles round the trees they fast enclose;
Sir Gawain, from the side of that burg was aware,
Shimmered the walls, and shone, thro' oaken branches bare.
Then swift he doffed his helm, thanking, I trow, that day
Christ, and Saint Julian, that they had heard alway
Courteous, his piteous prayer, and hearkened to his cry—
'Now grant me,' quoth the knight, 'here right good hostelry.'

Then pricked he Gringalet, with spurs of golden sheen,
The good steed chooseth well the chiefest gate, I
  ween.
And swift to the bridge end, he comes, the knight so
  keen,
  at last;
    The bridge aloft was stayed,
    The gates were shut full fast,
    The walls were well arrayed,
    They feared no tempest's blast.

XIII

The knight upon the bank his charger there doth stay,
Beyond the double ditch that round the castle lay,
The walls, in water set they were, and wondrous deep,
And high above his head it towered, the castle keep;
Of hard stone, fitly hewn, up to the corbels fair,
Beneath the battlements the stones well shapen were.
Above 't was fairly set with turrets in between,
And many a loop-hole fair for watchman's gaze so
  keen.
A better barbican had never met his eye—
Within, the knight beheld a goodly hall and high,
The towers set between the bristling battlements,
Round were they, shapen fair, of goodly ornament,
With carven capitals, by cunning craft well wrought,
Of chalk-white chimneys too, enow they were he
  thought.
On battled roof, arow, they shone, and glittered white,
And many a pinnacle adorned that palace bright.
The castle cornices they crownéd everywhere
So white and thick, it seemed they pared from paper
  were.

Gawain on Gringalet right good the castle thought
So he might find within the shelter that he sought,
And there, until the feast to fitting end were brought
  might rest,
   He called, a porter came,
   With fair speech, of the guest
   He craved from wall his name,
   And what were his behest?

XIV

'Good Sir,' then quoth Gawain, 'do thou for me this
  task,
Get thee unto thy lord, and say I shelter ask.'
'Nay, by Saint Peter good,' the porter quoth, ''t is well
Welcome be ye, Sir Knight, within these walls to dwell
Long as it liketh ye.' Then swift his way he went,
As swiftly came again, with folk on welcome bent.
The drawbridge let adown, from out the gate they
  came,
And on the ground so cold they knelt low at that
  same,
To welcome that good knight in worthy wise that tide;
They shew to him the gate with portals opened wide,
Then o'er the bridge he gat, with greeting gay, the
  knight,
Serjants his stirrups seize, and bid him swift alight.
To stable that good steed the men run readily,
The knights and squires, they come adown full
  speedily,
To bring that gentle knight with bliss unto the hall
Whenas he raised his helm they hasted one and all,
To take it from his hand, to serve him are they fain,

His goodly sword and shield, in charge they take the twain.
Then greeting good he gave those nobles, every one,
The proud men, pressing nigh, to him have honour done,
Still in his harness happed, to hall they lead him there,
Upon the floor there flamed a fire both fierce and fair,
The castle's lord doth come forth from his chamber door,
To greet, with fitting grace, his guest upon the floor.
He quoth: 'Be welcome here to stay as likes ye still,
For here all is your own to have at your own will,
    and hold—'
        'Gramercy,' quoth Gawain,
        'Of Christ be payment told,'
        In courteous wise the twain
        Embrace as heroes bold.

XV

Gawain gazed on the knight, who goodly greeting gave,
And deemed that burg so bright was owned of baron*brave,
For huge was he in height, and manhood's age he knew,
His broad beard on his breast, as beaver was its hue.
And stalwart in his stride, and strong, and straight, was he,
His face was red as fire, and frank his speech and free.
In sooth, Sir Gawain thought, 't would 'seem him well on land
To lead in lordship good of men a gallant band.

The lord, he led the way unto a chamber there,
And did his folk command to serve him fit and fair,
Then at his bidding came full many a gallant knight
They led him to a bower, with noble bedding dight.
The curtains all of silk, and hemmed with golden thread,
And comely coverings of fairest cloth o'er spread.
Above, of silk so bright, the broideries they were,
The curtains ran on ropes, with rings of red gold fair.
Rich tapestries of Tars, and Toulouse, on the wall
Hung fair, the floor was spread with the like cloth withal.
And there did they disarm, with many a mirthful rede,
The knight of byrnie bright, and of his warlike weed.
Then rich robes in their stead, I trow, they swiftly brought,
And for the change they chose the choicest to their thought.
Then soon he did them on, and I would have ye know,
Right well became the knight those skirts of seemly flow.
That hero, fair of face, he seeméd verily,
To all men who his mien and hue might nearer see
So sweet and lovesome there, of limb so light, they thought
That never Christ on earth a comelier had wrought—
That knight
    Thro' the world far and near
    Might well be deemed of right
    A prince with ne'er a peer
    In field of fiercest fight.

SIR GAWAIN AND THE GREEN KNIGHT

XVI

A chair before the fire of charcoal, burning bright,
They set for good Gawain, with cloth all draped and dight.
Cushion and footstool fit, the twain they were right good,
Then men a mantle cast around him as he stood,
'T was of a bliaunt brown, broidered in rich device,
And fairly furred within with pelts of goodly price,
Of whitest ermine all, and even so the hood.
Down in that seemly seat he sat, the gallant good,
And warmed him at the fire – then bettered was his cheer;
On trestles fairly set they fix a table near
And spread it with a cloth, that shewed all clean and white,
Napkin and salt-cellar with silver spoons so bright.
The knight washed at his will, and set him down to eat,
Serjants, they served him there in seemly wise and meet;
With diverse dishes sweet, and seasoned of the best,
A double portion then they set before the guest,
Of fishes, baked in bread, or broiled on glowing wood,
Anon came fishes seethed, or stewed with spices good,
With choicest dainties there, as pleasing to his taste—
The knight, he quoth full oft, a feast that board had graced,
Then all, as with one voice, this answer made in haste:
'Fair Friend,
    This penance shall ye take,
    It shall ye well amend!'
    Much mirth the knight did make
    For wine did gladness lend.

TRANSLATED BY JESSIE WESTON

XVII

The hosts, in courteous wise the truth are fain to know
Of this, their goodly guest, if he his name will shew?
As courteously he quoth, he from that court did fare
Holden of good renown, where Arthur rule did bear,
(Rich, royal king was he) o'er all the Table Round—
And 't was Gawain himself who here had haven found,
Hither for Christmas come, as chance had ruled it right
Then when the lord had learned he had for guest that knight
Loudly he laughed for joy, he deemed such tidings good—
All men within the moat they waxed of mirthful mood
To think that they that tide should in his presence be
Who, for his prowess prized, and purest courtesie,
That doth to him belong, was praiséd everywhere,
Of all men upon earth none might with him compare.
Each to his fellow said, full softly, 'Now shall we
The seemly fashion fair of courts full fitly see,
With faultless form of speech, and trick of noble word,
What charm in such may be that shall, unasked, be heard
Since here the father fine of courtesie we greet.
Methinks Christ sheweth us much grace, and favour meet,
In granting us such guest for Yule as good Gawain:
When men, blithe for His birth, to sit, methinks, are fain,
   and sing,
      Customs of courtesie
      This knight to us shall teach

> And from his lips maybe
> We'll learn of love the speech.'

XVIII

> By that was dinner done, the knight from table rose,
> The eventide drew nigh, the day was near its close,
> The chosen chaplains there to chapel go forthright,
> Loudly the bells they ring, e'en as was fit and right.
> To solemn evensong of this High Feast they go—
> The lord the prayers would hear, his lady fair also,
> To comely closet closed she entereth straightway;
> And even so, full soon, follows Sir Gawain gay.
> The lord his lappet took, and led him to a seat,
> Hailing him by his name, in guise of friendship meet,
> Of all knights in the world was he most welcome there
> He thanked him, and the twain embrace with kisses fair,
> And soberly they sit throughout the service high—
> Then 't was the lady's will to see that knight with eye,
> With many a maiden fair she cometh from her place,
> Fairest was she in skin, in figure, and in face,
> Of height and colour too, in every way so fair
> That e'en Gaynore, the queen, might scarce with her compare.
> She thro' the chancel came, to greet that hero good,
> Led by another dame, who at her left hand stood;
> Older she was, I trow, and reverend seemingly,
> With goodly following of nobles, verily;
> But all unlike to sight, I trow, those ladies were,
> Yellow, the older dame, whereas the first was fair.
> The cheeks of one were red, e'en as the rose doth glow,
> The other, wrinkles rough, in plenty, did she shew.

The younger, kerchiefs soft, with many a pearl so white,
Ware, that her breast and throat full well displayed to sight,
Whiter they were than snow that on the hills doth lie—
The other's neck was veiled in gorget folded high,
That all her chin so black was swathed in milk-white folds;
Her forehead all, I ween, in silk was rapped and rolled,
Broidered it was full fair, adorned with knots enow,
Till naught of her was seen save the black bristly brow.
Her eyes, her nose, I ween, and eke her lips, were bare
And those were ill to see, so bleared and sour they were—
Meet mistress upon mold, so men might her declare that tide—
    Short and thick-set was she,
    Her hips were broad and wide,
    And fairer far to see
    The lady at her side.

XIX

When Gawain saw that dame, gracious of mien, and gay,
Leave from his host he craved, and t'wards her took his way;
The elder, bowing low, he fittingly doth greet,
Lightly within his arms he folds the lady sweet
Gives her a comely kiss, as fit from courteous knight;

She hailed him as her friend – a boon he prays
  forthright,
Her servant would he be, an so her will it were—
Betwixt the twain he walks, and, talking still, they fare
To hall, and e'en to hearth, and at the lord's command
Spices in plenty great are ready to their hand,
With wine that maketh gay at feast time, as is meet—
The lord, in laughing wise, he sprang unto his feet,
Bade them make mirth enow – all men his words
  must hear—
His hood he doffed from head, and hung it on a spear,
And quoth that that same man worship thereof should
  win
Who made the greatest mirth that Christmas-tide
  within:
'I'll fail not, by my faith, to frolic with the best,
Ere that my hood I lose – with help of every guest.'
And thus, with joyous jest the lord doth try withal
To gladden Sir Gawain with games in this his hall
  that night;
    Till that the torches' flare
    He needs must bid them light,
    Gawain must from them fare
    And seek his couch forthright.

XX

Then, on the morrow morn, when all men bear in
  mind
How our dear Lord was born to die for all mankind,
Joy in each dwelling dwells, I wot well, for His sake,
So did it there that day, when men High Feast would
  make;
For then, at every meal, messes, full richly dressed,

Men served upon the dais, with dainties of the best;
That ancient lady there doth fill the highest seat,
The castle's lord, I trow, beside her, as was meet.
Sir Gawain hath his place beside that lady gay
At midmost of the board, when meat was served alway.
And then, thro' all the hall, each one, as seemed him best,
Sat, each in his degree – fitly they served each guest,
Much meat had they and mirth, with joy and merry song,
Methinks to tell thereof would take me over-long
Altho' perchance I strove to tell that tale as meet—
I wot well that Gawain, and this, the lady sweet,
In their fair fellowship much comfort needs must find,
In the dear dalliance of words and glances kind,
And converse courteous, from all unfitness free—
Such pastime fitting were for prince in purity—
   Sweet strain
      Of trump and piping clear
      And drum, doth sound amain;
      Each doth his minstrel hear,
      And even so the twain.

XXI

Much mirth they made that day, and e'en the morrow's morn
Nor slackened of the feast when the third day was born;
The joy of sweet Saint John, gentle it was to hear,
The folk, they deemed the feast fast to its end drew near;

SIR GAWAIN AND THE GREEN KNIGHT

(The guests must needs depart, e'en in the dawning grey)
Full early did they rise, and serve the wine straightway;
Danced carols merrily, so, blithe, the day they passed,
And when the hour waxed late they took their leave at last.
Each one to wend his way whenas the day should break—
Gawain would bid good-day – his hand the lord doth take
To his own chamber leads, and by the chimney wide,
To thank his guest full fain, he draweth him aside;
Thanks him for worship fair that he from him had won,
And for the honour high he to his house had done
By lending countenance unto this Christmas Feast—
'Of honours, while I live, I'll count this not the least
That Gawain this, my guest, at Christ's own Feast hath been!'
'Gramercy,' quoth Gawain, 'In all good faith, I ween
The honour it is yours, and may Christ you repay.
I wait upon your word, to do your will alway
As I be bound thereto by night and e'en by day
of right—'
    The lord, he was full fain
    To keep with him the knight,
    Then answered him Gawain
    That he in no wise might.

XXII

The lord, he courteous prayed that he would tell him there
What deed of daring drove Gawain afar to fare

TRANSLATED BY JESSIE WESTON

E'en at this time from court, and thus alone to wend,
Before this Holy Feast had come unto an end?
'In sooth, Sir,' quoth the knight, 'Ye speak the truth alway,
A hasty quest, and high, doth send me on my way,
For I myself must seek, and find, a certain place
And whitherward to wend I wot not, by God's grace!
Nor would I miss my tryst at New Year, by my soul,
For all the land of Logres! Christ help me to my goal!
Therefore Sir Host, I now require ye without fail
To tell me here in truth if ye e'er heard a tale
Told of a Chapel Green? Where such a place may be?
The knight who keepeth it, green too, I ween, is he;
We sware a forward fast, I trow, between us twain,
That I that man would meet, might I thereto attain,
And to that same New Year but few days now remain—
Now fainer far would I behold that self-same knight,
If so it were God's will, than any gladder sight;
Therefore with your good will, I needs must wend my way
Since I have, for my quest, but three bare days alway;
Fainer were I to die than fail in this my quest—'
Then, laughing, quoth the lord: 'Of needs must be my guest,
I'll shew to thee thy goal ere yet the term be o'er
That very Chapel Green – so vex thy soul no more,
Do thou in bed abide and take thine ease, I pray,
Until the fourth day dawn, with New Year go thy way
And thou shalt reach thy goal ere yet it be midday.
   So, still,
      To the New Year abide
      Then rise, thy goal is near
      Men shall thee thither guide,
      'T is not two miles from here—'

XXIII

Sir Gawain, he was glad, and laughed out gay and free,
'I thank ye, Sire, for this, o'er all your courtesie,
Achieved is this my quest, and I shall, at your will
Within your burg abide, and do your pleasure still.'
The lord, he took that knight, and set him at his side,
And bade the ladies come to cheer them at that tide,
Tho' they had, of themselves, fair solace, verily—
The host, for very joy, he jested merrily
As one for meed of mirth scarce wist what he might say.
Then, turning to the knight, he cried on him alway:
'Didst swear to do the deed I should of thee request,
Now art thou ready here to hearken my behest?'
'Yea, Sire, forsooth am I,' so quoth that hero true
'While in your burg I bide, servant am I to you!'
'Now,' quoth the host, 'methinks, your travail sore hath been,
Here hast thou waked with me, nor had thy fill, I ween,
Of sustenance, or sleep, – an thou thine host wouldst please
Thou shalt lie long in bed, and, lingering, take thine ease
At morn, nor rise for mass, but eat as thou shalt say
E'en when thou wilt, my wife with thee a while shall stay
And solace thee with speech, till I my homeward way have found.
    For I betimes shall rise,
    A-hunting am I bound.'
    Gawain, this, his device
    Doth grant him at that stound.

TRANSLATED BY JESSIE WESTON

XXIV

'First,' quoth the host, 'we'll make a forward fair and free,
Whate'er in wood I win the profit thine shall be,
What cheer thou shalt achieve, shalt give me, 'gainst my gain;
Now swear me here with truth to keep this 'twixt us twain
Whate'er our hap may be, or good or ill befall.—'
'By God,' quoth good Gawain, 'I grant ye this withal,
An such play pleaseth you, forsooth it pleaseth me—'
'Now, bring the beverage here, the bargain set shall be.'
So quoth the castle's lord, and each one laughed, I trow,
They drank and dallied there and dealt with sport enow,
Those lords and ladies fair, e'en as it liked them best,
And so, in friendship fair, with many a courteous jest,
They stood, and stayed awhile, and spake with softest speech,
Then kissed at parting, e'en as courtesy doth teach.
And then, with service fit, and many a torch alight,
Unto his bed at last they brought each gallant knight again—
  Yet ere their couch they sought
  The cov'nant 'twixt the twain
  The lord to memory brought,
  For jesting was he fain.

Book III

I

Full early ere 't was day the folk arise withal,
The guests would go their way – upon their grooms
  they call,
They busk them busily to saddle each good steed,
The girths they tighten there, and truss the mails at
  need.
The nobles, ready all, in riding gear arrayed,
Leapt lightly to their steeds, their hand on bridle laid;
Each wight upon his way doth at his will ride fast—
The lord of all the land, I wot, was not the last,
Ready for riding he, with his men, at that same
Ate a sop hastily whenas from mass they came.
With blast of bugle bold forth upon bent he 'ld go,
Ere yet the day had dawned on the cold earth below.
He and his knights bestrode, each one, their horses
  high.
The huntsmen couple then the hounds right speedily.
Then, calling on the dogs, unclose the kennel door;
A bugle blast they blow, but three notes, and no more.
Loudly the brachets bay, and wake the echoes there,

They check their hounds so good who to the chase
  would fare
A hundred men all told, so doth the tale declare
  ride fast;
    The trackers on the trail
    The hounds, uncoupled, cast,
    Thro' forest, hill and dale
    Rings loud the bugle blast.

II

At the first warning note that bade the hunt awake
The deer within the dale for dread they needs must
  quake;
Swift to the heights they hie – but soon must turn
  about,
The men in ambush hid so loud they cry and shout.
The harts, with heads high-held, they pass in safety
  there,
E'en so the stately stags with spreading antlers fair,
(For so the lords' command at close time of the year
That none should lift his hand save 'gainst the female
  deer.)
The hinds with '*Hag*' and '*War*' they hold the lines
  within,
The does are driven back to dale with deafening din;
Swift as they speed, I trow, fair shooting might ye see,
The arrows striking true as 'neath the boughs they
  flee;
Their broad heads deeply wound, and, smitten on the
  flank,
The bleeding deer they fall, dying, upon the bank.
The hounds, in hasty course, follow upon the trail,

Huntsmen, with sounding horns, for speed they do not fail,
Follow with ringing cries that cliffs might cleave in twain;
The deer that 'scape the darts, they by the dogs are ta'en,
Run down, and riven, and rent, within the bounds so wide,
Harassed upon the hill, worried by waterside;
The men well knew their craft of forest and of flood,
The greyhounds were full swift to follow thro' the wood,
They caught them ere the men with arrows, as they stood,
   could smite—
      The lord was glad and gay,
      His lance he wielded light,
      With joy he passed the day
      Till fell the shades of night.

III

The lord, he maketh sport beneath the woodland bough,
Sir Gawain, that good knight, in bed he lieth now,
Hiding, while daylight gleamed upon the walls without,
'Neath costly cov'ring fair, curtained all round about.
As he half slumbering lay, it seeméd to his ear
A small sound at his door all sudden must he hear;
His head a little raised above the covering soft,
He grasps the curtain's edge, and lifteth it aloft,
And waiteth warily to wot what fate may hold—
It was the lady fair, most lovely to behold!

TRANSLATED BY JESSIE WESTON

Gently she drew the door behind her, closing tight,
And came toward the couch – shamed was that gallant knight,
He laid him lightly down, and made as tho' he slept;
So stole she to his side, and light and soft she stept,
The curtain upward cast, within its fold she crept,
And there upon his bed her seat she soft doth take
Waiting in patience still until that he awake.
Cautious and quiet, awhile the knight, half hidden, lay,
And in his conscience conned the case with care alway;
What might the meaning be? He marvelled much, I trow,
Yet quoth within himself: 'It were more seemly now
To speak with gentle speech, ask what her will may be,
So made he feint to wake, and turned him presently
Lifted his eyelids then, and stared, as in amaze,
Made of the Cross the sign, that so his words and ways be wise—

    Her chin and cheeks are sweet
    In red and white devise,
    Gracious, she doth him greet
    With laughing lips and eyes.

IV

'Good-morrow, Sir Gawain,' so spake the lady fair,
'A careless sleeper ye, I came ere ye were ware,
Now are ye trapped and ta'en, as ye shall truly know,
I'll bind ye in your bed ere that ye hence should go!'
Laughing, the lady lanced her jests at him alway,

SIR GAWAIN AND THE GREEN KNIGHT

Sir Gawain answered blithe: 'Give ye good-morrow gay,
Know I am at your will, (forsooth it pleaseth me)
And here for grace I yearn, yielding me readily.
For where one needs must yield to do so swift were best!'
And thus he answer made, with many a merry jest;
'But might I, Lady fair, find grace before your eyes,
Then loose, I pray, your bonds, and bid your prisoner rise,
I'd get me from this bed, and better clad, I trow,
I in your converse kind comfort would find enow.'
'Nay, nay, forsooth, beau Sire,' so quoth that lady sweet,
'Ye shall not rise from bed, I'll rede ye counsel meet,
For I shall hold ye here, since other may not be,
And talk with this my knight, who captive is to me,
For well I know, in sooth, ye are that same Gawain
Worshipped by all the world where ye to fare be fain;
For all your honour praise, your gracious courtesie,
Or lords or ladies fair, all men on earth that be!
Now are ye here, I wis, and all alone we twain,
My lord to fare afield with his free folk is fain,
The men, they lie abed, so do my maidens all—
The door is safely shut, and closed and hasped withal;
Since him whom all men praise I in my hand hold fast,
I well will use my time the while the chance doth last!
    Now rest,
        My body's at your will
        To use as ye think best,
        Perforce, I find me still
        Servant to this my guest!'

TRANSLATED BY JESSIE WESTON

V

'In good faith,' quoth Gawain, 'I now bethink me well,
I be not such an one as this your tale would tell!
To reach such reverence as ye rehearse but now
I all unworthy were – that do I soothly vow!
Yet, God wot, I were glad, an so ye thought it good,
If I in word and deed here at your service stood;
To pleasure this your prayer, a pure joy 't were to me.'
'In good faith, Sir Gawain,' the lady answered free,
'The prowess and the praise that please us ladies fair
I lack not, nor hold light, but little gain it were
Ladies there be enow to whom it were more dear
To hold their knight in hold, e'en as I hold ye here,
To dally daintily with courteous words and fair
That bring them comfort good, and cure them of their care,
Than wealth of treasure told, or gold they own withal—
But now I praise the Lord who here upholdeth all
Him whom they all desire is in my hold and hall
  of grace!'
    She made him such good cheer
    That lady fair of face,
    The knight was fain to hear
    And answer, in his place.

VI

He quoth: 'Now Mary Maid reward ye, as she may,
I find your frankness fair and noble, sooth to say.
Full many folk, I trow, have well entreated me,
Yet greater honour far than all their courtesie

SIR GAWAIN AND THE GREEN KNIGHT

I count your praise, who naught save goodness here
  shall know.'
'By Mary Maid,' she quoth, 'methinks it is not so,
For were my worth above all women who may live,
And all of this world's wealth were in mine hand to
  give,
And I were free of choice a lord to choose to me,
Then, for the customs good I in this knight must see,
For beauty debonaire, for bearing blithe and gay,
For all that I have heard, and hold for truth alway,
Upon no man on mold save ye my choice were laid.'
'I wot well,' quoth the knight, 'a better choice ye
  made!
Yet am I proud of this, the praise, ye give to me,
My sovereign ye, and I your servant, verily,
Do yield me here your knight, and may Christ ye
  repay!'
They spake of many things till noon had passed away,
And aye the lady made mien that she loved him well,
And aye he turned aside her sweet words as they fell,
For were she brightest maid of maidens to his mind,
The less love would he shew, since loss he thought to
  find
  anon—
    The blow that should him slay,
    And for his blow was boon—
    The lady leave did pray.
    He granted her, full soon.

VII

Then, as she gave 'good-day,' she laughed with glance
  so gay,
And, standing, spake a word that 'stonied him alway:

TRANSLATED BY JESSIE WESTON

'May He who speedeth speech reward thee well, I trow,
But that ye be Gawain I much misdoubt me now,'—
'And wherefore?' quoth the knight in fashion frank and fair
Fearing lest he have failed in custom debonaire:
The lady blessed him then, and spake as in this wise:
'Gawain so good a knight is holden in all eyes,
So clad in courtesie is he, in sooth, that ne'er
Had he thus holden speech for long with lady fair
But he had craved a kiss by this, his courtesie,
Or trifling token ta'en at end of converse free!'
Then quoth Gawain: 'Ywis, if this ye fitting deem
I'll kiss at your command, as doth a knight beseem
Who tarrieth to ask, and doth refusal fear—'
She clasped him in her arms, e'en as she stood anear,
Lightly she bent adown, and kissed that knight so free,
Commending him to Christ, as he her, courteously—
Then, without more ado, forth from the door she went;
The knight made haste to rise, on speed was he intent,
He called his chamberlain, his robes he chose anon,
When he was fitly garbed to mass he blithe has gone;
Then sat him down to meat, 't was served in fitting guise,
Merry he passed the day, and, till the moon did rise made game—

    Better was never knight
    Entreated of fair dame
    Old, or of beauty bright,
    Than he was, at that same.

VIII

And aye the lord in land finds sport unto his mind,
Hunting o'er hill and heath, chasing the barren hind,
So many hath he slain, ere yet the sun was low,
Of does, and other deer, a wonder 't was to know.
The folk together flock, whenas the end drew near
Quickly a quarry make of all the slaughtered deer;
The best, they bowed thereto, with many a knight to aid,
The fairest hinds of grease together they have laid,
Set them to quartering there, e'en as the need doth ask,
The fat was set aside by those who knew their task,
From all uncleanness freed, the flesh they sever there,
The chest they slit, and draw the erber forth with care;
With knife both sharp and keen the neck they next divide,
Then sever all four limbs, and strip off fair the hide.
The belly open slit, the bowels aside they lay,
With swift strokes of the knife the knot they cut away;
They grip the gargiloun, and speedily divide
Weasand and wind-pipe then, the guts are cast aside,
The shoulder-blade around, with blade so sharp and keen,
They cut, and leave the side whole and untouched, I ween.
The breast they deftly carve, the halves they lie a-twin,
And with the gargiloun their work they now begin;
They rip it swiftly up, and take it clean away,
Void the avancers out, and then, methinks, straightway
The skin betwixt the ribs they cut in fashion fair

Till they have left them all e'en to the backbone bare.
So come they to the haunch, that doth belong thereto,
They bear it up all whole, and cleanly cut it thro'
That, with the numbles, take, alike they be the two,
  of kind
    Then, where the thighs divide
    The flaps they cut behind,
    And thus, on either side,
    Thighs from the back unbind.

IX

Then head and neck alike, they hew them off with
  heed,
The sides from off the chine are sundered now with
  speed.
The corbie's fee they cast into the wood hard by,
Each thick side thro' the ribs they pierce it, verily,
And hang them all aloft, fixed to the haunches fair—
Each fellow for his fee doth take as fitting there.
Then, on a deer's skin spread, they give the hounds
  their food.
The liver, lights, and paunch, to keep the custom
  good,
And bread soaked in the blood they scatter 'mid the
  pack—
The hounds, they bay amain, nor bugle blast doth
  lack.
Thus, with the venison good, they take the homeward
  way,
Sounding upon their horns a merry note and gay.
By that, the day was done, the folk, with eventide,
That comely castle sought, wherein their guest doth
  bide

full still—
> To bliss and firelight bright
> The lord is come at will;
> To meet that goodly knight—
> Of joy they had their fill!

X

Then at the lord's command, the folk they thither call,
Quickly the ladies come, and maidens, one and all,
And there before the folk he bids his men straightway,
The venison they have brought before them all to lay.
And then, in goodly jest, he calleth Sir Gawain,
The tale of that day's sport he to rehearse is fain,
Shews him how fair the fat upon the ribs, sharp shorn,
And quoth: 'How seemeth this? Have I won praise this morn?
Am I, thro' this my craft, worthy of praise from thee?'
'Yea, soothly,' quoth Gawain, 'the fairest game I see
That I in winter-time have seen this seven year!'
'And all this,' quoth his host, 'Gawain, I give thee here
By covenant and accord, the whole thou well may'st claim.'
''T is sooth,' then said the knight, 'I grant ye at this same.
Won have I worthily a prize, these walls within
Which, with as good a will, ye now from me must win.'
With that he clasps his arms around his neck so fair
And in right comely wise he kissed him then and there,
'Now here hast thou my gain, no more hath fallen to me—
I trow had it been more my gift were none less free!'

"'T is good,' quoth the good knight, 'nor shall my
   thanks be slow
Yet might it better be, an I the truth might know,
Where thou didst win this grace, or by thy wit or no?'
'Ask no more,' quoth Gawain, 'so did our forward
   stand,'
Since ye have ta'en your right no more may ye
   demand.'
   At will
      They laughed and made them gay
      With many a jest I trow,
      To supper go straightway,
      With dainties new enow.

XI

Then by the hearth they sit, on silken cushions soft,
And wine, within those walls, I wot, they serve full
   oft,
And, ever, as they jest, come morrow morn, they say
That forward they'll fulfil which they had kept to-day.
What chance soe'er betide, they will exchange their
   gain
When they at nightfall meet, be much or little ta'en.
This covenant they accord, in presence of the court,
And beverage to the board at that same time was
   brought,
A courteous leave, at last, doth each from other take,
And each man for his bed himself doth ready make.
The cock at early morn, had crowed and cackled thrice
When swift, the lord arose, with him his knights of
   price;
They hearken mass, and meat, with service fit, they
   bring,

Then forth to forest fare ere yet the day doth spring
  for chace—
    With sound of hunter's horns
    O'er plain they swiftly pace,
    Uncoupled midst the thorns
    Each hound doth run on race.

XII

Full soon they strike the scent, hard by a rock withal,
Huntsmen cheer on those hounds who first upon it
  fall,
Loudly, with whirling words, and clamour rising high,
The hounds that heard the call haste hither at the cry.
Fast on the scent they fall, full forty at that tide,
Till of the pack the cry was heard both far and wide.
So fiercely rose their bay, the rocks, they rang again,
The huntsmen with their horns to urge them on were
  fain.
Then, sudden, all the pack together crowd and cry
Before a thicket dense, beneath a crag full high,
Hard by the water's edge – the pack, with one
  consent,
Run to the rugged rocks, which lie all scarred and
  rent.
Hounds to the finding fare, the men, they follow keen,
And cast about the crag, and rocks that lie between.
The knights, full well they knew what beast had here
  its lair
And fain would drive it forth before the bloodhounds
  there.
Then on the bush they beat, and bid the game uprise—
With sudden rush across the beaters, out there hies
A great and grisly boar, most fearsome to behold,

The herd he long had left, for that he waxed full old.
Of beast, and boar, methinks, biggest and fiercest he,
I trow me at his grunt full many grieved must be;
Three at the first assault prone on the earth he threw,
And sped forth at best speed, nor other harm they knew.
Then Hey! and Hey! the knights halloo with shout and cry,
Huntsmen with horn to mouth send forth shrill notes and high,
Merry the noise of men and dogs, I ween, that tide
Who followed on the boar – with boastful shout they cried
   to stay—
      The hounds' wrath would he quell
      Oft as he turned to bay,
      Loudly they yelp and yell,
      His tusks they tare alway.

XIII

The men make ready then their arrows sharp and keen,
The darts they swiftly fly, oft is he hit, I ween,
But never point may pierce, nor on his hide have hold,
And never barb may bite his forehead's fearsome fold.
The shafts are splintered there, shivered, they needs must fall,
The heads, they bit indeed, yet but rebound withal.
But when he felt the blows, tho' harmless all they fell,
Then, mad for rage, he turned, and 'venged him passing well;
He rushed upon the knights, and wounded them full sore

Until, for very fear, they fled his face before.
The lord, on steed swift-paced, doth follow on his track,
Blowing his bugle loud, nor valour doth he lack,
Thus thro' the wood he rides, his horn rings loud and low,
Upon the wild boar's track until the sun was low.
And so the winter's day he passeth on this wise
The while his goodly guest in bed, 'neath covering lies,
Sir Gawain bides at home – In gear of rich devise and hue,
    The dame made no delay
    To greet her knight so true,
    Early she took her way
    To test his mood anew.

XIV

She to the curtain comes, and looks upon the knight,
Gawain doth greet her there in fitting wise and right;
She greeteth him again, ready of speech is she,
Soft seats her at his side, and laughs full merrily.
Then, with a smiling glance these words to him doth say:
'Sir, an ye be Gawain I marvel much alway,
So stern ye be when one would goodly ye entreat,
Of courteous company ignore the customs meet,
An one be fain to teach, swift from your mind they're brought
Since all forgotten now what yesterday I taught
By truest tokens all, that well might be, I trow.'
'What is that?' quoth Gawain, 'naught I remember now,

TRANSLATED BY JESSIE WESTON

But if 't is sooth ye speak, then blame I needs must
    bear.'
'Of kissing was my rede'; so quoth the lady fair,
'When countenance be known, swiftly a kiss to claim,
That doth become a knight who beareth courteous
    name!'
'Nay, cease, my dear, such speech,' so quoth the
    gallant knight,
'A kiss I dare not claim, lest ye deny my right,
For an ye did forbid, to take, I trow, were wrong—
'I' faith,' in merry wise she spake, 'ye be too strong,
Ye may not be forbid, since ye may take with might
An any do such wrong as to deny thy right!'
'Yea,' quoth Gawain, 'by Christ, your speech it
    soundeth well,
But threats shall little thrive in that land where I
    dwell,
Nor count we fair a gift that is not proffered free—
I am at your command, to kiss, if so shall be
Your will – to take or leave, as seemeth good to ye.'
    With grace,
        She bent, that lady fair,
        And gently kissed his face.
        They hold sweet converse there,
        Of love-themes speak a space.

XV

'Fain would I ask of ye, (that lady questioned free)
If so ye were not wroth, what may the reason be
That one so young and fair, as ye be at this tide,
For knightly courtesie renowned both far and wide,
Who of all chivalry the head and chief men hold,

Versed in the lore of love, and warfare, fierce and
  bold—
Since each true knight doth tell how he did venture
  dare
(This token and this sign his deeds perforce must bear)
How for a lady's love his life at stake he set,
And for her favour fair full doleful dints hath met,
With valour 'venged her wrongs, and cured her of her
  care
Brought bliss unto her bower, and did her bounties
  share—
And ye be comeliest knight of this, your land and
  time,
Your worship and your words be famed in every clime,
And I, two mornings long have sat beside ye here
Yet never from your mouth a word came to mine ear
That ever dealt with love, in measure less or more;
But ye, so courteous held, so skilled in all such lore,
Surely to one so young as I should swiftly shew
And teach some token sure, whereby true love to
  know.
Are ye unlearnéd then, whom men so highly prize?
Or am I all too dull for dalliance, in your eyes?
  For shame!
    Hither I come and sit
    To learn, as at this same;
    So teach me of your wit,
    While sport my lord doth claim!'

XVI

'In good faith,' quoth Gawain, 'your good deeds God
  repay,
For goodly is my glee, my profit great alway;

That one so fair as ye doth deign betake ye here
To please so poor a man, and me, your knight, to cheer
With kindly countenance, in sooth doth please me well
But that I, in my turn, should here of true love tell,
And take that for my theme, (or tales of gallant knight)
And teach ye, who I wot, doth wield more skilful sleight
In such arts by the half, or hundred-fold indeed,
Than I, long as I live on earth may win for meed,
'T were folly all indeed, sweet lady, by my fay!
Your will in troth I'll work in such wise as I may,
As duteous I am bound – and ever more will do
Your service faithfully, God grant me grace thereto!'
Thus did she ask him fair, and oft did test and try,
To win him here to woo, whate'er her will thereby—
But he doth fend him fair, nor ill hath done, I ween,
And never deed of wrong hath chanced the twain between,
  but bliss—
    They laugh and talk amain,
    At last she doth him kiss,
    Her leave of him hath ta'en,
    And gone her way, I wis.

XVII

Then doth Sir Gawain rise, and robe him, mass to hear.
Then was the dinner dight, and served with mickle cheer;
Thus, with the ladies twain, in sport the day he spent,
The while the lord doth chase the boar o'er bank and bent—

SIR GAWAIN AND THE GREEN KNIGHT

Follows the grisly swine, as o'er the holts it sped,
With broken back, his hounds, beneath its jaws fall dead.
The boar would bide at bay, the bowmen grant no grace,
But force him 'gainst his will once more his foes to face.
So fast the arrows fly, the folk they gather round,
Yet huntsmen stiff and stern, he startles at that stound.
Till spent with flight, at last, he may no further win,
But hies him in all haste, until a hole within
A mound, beside a rock, hard by the brooklet's flow,
He gains – then turns at bay, tearing the ground below.
His jaws, they foam and froth, unseemly to behold,
He whets his tusks so white – was never man so bold
Of those who faced him there, who dare the issue try;
They eye him from afar, but none will venture nigh.
    Right wroth,
        Many he smote before,
        Thus all might well be loath
        To face the tusks that tore—
        So mad was he, i' troth.

XVIII

Then cometh swift the lord, spurring his goodly steed,
See'th the boar at bay, of his men taketh heed;
He lighteth from his horse, leaves it with hanging rein,
Draws out his blade so bright, and strideth forth amain.
Fast does he ford the stream, the boar bides on the strand,

TRANSLATED BY JESSIE WESTON

'Ware of the gallant wight, with weapon fast in hand;
His bristles rise amain, grim were his snarls withal,
The folk were sore afraid, lest harm their lord befall.
The swine, with spring so swift, upon the hero fell,
That boar and baron bold none might asunder tell,
There, in the water deep, the boar, he had the worst,
For the man marked him well, e'en as they met at first,
His sharp blade in the slot he set, e'en to the heft,
And, driving hard and true, the heart asunder cleft,
Snarling, he yields his hold, the stream him hence hath reft.
    Forthright,
        The hounds, with fierce onslaught
        Fall to, the boar they bite,
        Swift to the shore he's brought,
        And dogs to death him dight.

XIX

Forthwith from many a horn a joyful blast they blow,
Huntsmen together vie, high rings the loud 'Hallo!'
The brachets bay their best, e'en at their masters' will,
Who in that fearsome chace had proved their hunters' skill.
And then a wight so wise in woodcraft, fit and fair,
The quarry to unlace hath set him straightway there.
He heweth off the head, and setteth it on high,
With skill he rendeth down the backbone, presently,
Then, bringing forth the bowels, roasts them on embers red,
And, to reward his hounds, doth blend them with their bread.
He strippeth off the brawn, e'en as in shields it were,

The hastlets hath he ta'en, and drawn them forth with
  care.
The halves he taketh now, and binds them as a whole,
With withy stiff and stout, made fast unto a pole.
And with that self-same swine homeward they fare
  thro' land;
The boar's head do they bear before their lord, on
  brand,
Who slew him in the ford, by force of his right hand
  so strong—
> Till he might see Gawain
> In hall, he deemed it long,
> His guest he was full fain
> To pay, nor do him wrong.

XX

The lord, with merry jest, and laugh of gladsome glee
Soon as he saw Gawain, spake words both fair and
  free,
(The ladies too he bade, e'en with the household all—)
The boar's shields doth he show, and tells his tale
  withal,
How broad he was, how long, how savage in his mood,
That grisly swine – and how they chased him thro' the
  wood,
Sir Gawain doth commend his deeds, in comely wise,
Well hath he proved himself, to win so fair a prize—
'For such a brawny beast, (so spake that baron bold)
And such shields of a swine, mine eyes did ne'er
  behold.'
They handle the huge head, the knight doth praise it
  well,

TRANSLATED BY JESSIE WESTON

And loud and fair his speech, his host his mind may tell.
'Gawain,' quoth the good man, 'this gain is sure your own,
By forward fair and fast, e'en as before was shown.'
'Yea,' quoth the knight, ''t is true, and here too, by my troth,
I give ye all my gain, nor thereto am I loth.'
With that he clasped his host, and doth him kindly kiss,
And so a second time he did the same, I wis.
'Now are we,' quoth Gawain, 'quit in this eventide
Of forwards all we made since I with ye abide
in hall.'
    The lord quoth: 'By Saint Giles,
    I hold ye best withal,
    Rich are ye in short, while
    Your profits be not small!'

XXI

The tables then they bring, on trestles set aloft,
And cover them as meet, with cloths both fair and soft,
Clear falleth on the walls, of waxen torch, the light;
Sithen, to service fair they set them, many a knight.
Then clamour glad, and glee, arose within the hall,
Where flares the flame on floor they make much mirth withal,
They sing, e'en as they sup, and after, knights so true,
Fair songs of Christmas-tide, and many a carol new,
With every kind of mirth that man to tell were fain—
And by that lady's side he sat, the good Gawain,

Such semblance fair she made, in seemly wise and meet,
To please the gentle knight, with stolen glances sweet,
Whereat he marvelled much, and chid himself amain,
Yet, for his courtesy, would answer not again,
Dealing in dainty wise, till fate the die was fain
  to cast.
    Thus made they mirth in hall,
    Long as their will did last,
    Then, when the lord did call,
    To chimney-corner passed.

XXII

They drank, and dallied, there, and deemed 't were well to hold
Their forward fast and fair till New Year's Eve were told,
But Gawain prayed his leave, with morrow's morn to ride,
Since it were nigh the term his challenge to abide.
The lord withheld his leave, praying him strait to stay:
'As I be faithful knight, I pledge my troth alway
Thou shalt thy tryst fulfil, there at the Chapel Green,
Before the New Year's Morn hath waxed to prime, I ween;
So lie, and rest thee soft, and take thine ease at will,
And I shall hunt the holts, and keep our forward still,
To change my gain with thee, all that I homeward bear—
Twice have I tested thee, and found thee true and fair,
A third time will we try our luck, at dawn of day;
Now think ye upon joy, be merry while ye may,
For men may laugh at loss, if so their will alway.'

Gawain doth grant the grace, and saith, he will abide;
Blithely they brought him drink, and then to bed they hied
  with light—
    Sir Gawain lies and sleeps
    Soft, thro' the stilly night,
    The lord his cov'nant keeps,
    For chase is early dight.

XXIII

A morsel after mass, he taketh with his men,
Merry the morning tide – his mount he prayeth then,
They who, a-horse, should hold him company that day
A-saddle all, their steeds before the hall-gate stay.
Full fair it was a-field, the frost yet fast doth cling,
Ruddy, and red, the sun its rising beams doth fling,
And clear, and cloudless all, appears the welkin wide—
The huntsmen scatter them hard by a woodland side,
The rocks, they rang again before the horn's loud blast,
Some fell upon a track, where late a fox had passed—
(The trail may oft betray, tho' fox no feint doth lack—)
A hound hath found the scent, the hunt is on his track,
The dogs, they follow fast, and thick the hue and cry,
They run in rabble rout on the trail speedily
The fox, he fled apace, the hounds their prey have seen,
And, once within their sight, they follow fast and keen,
Loudly they threaten there, with cry and clamour fierce

The fox, with twist and turn, the undergrowth doth pierce,
Winding, and hearkening oft, low thro' the hedge doth creep,
Then, by a little ditch, doth o'er a spinney leap,
So, still, he stealeth forth, by rough and rugged way
Thinking to clear the wood, and cheat the hounds that day;
Then, ere he wist, I trow, to hunters' tryst he came
Threatened he was threefold, by hounds as at that same:
    from fray
        He starteth swift aside,
        And fled, as he were fey;
        Fain was he at that tide
        To seek the woodland way.

XXIV

'T was lively then to list the hounds, as loud they cry,
When all the pack had met, and mingled, speedily,
Such wrath, methinks, adown upon his head they call
As all the climbing cliffs had clashed unto their fall.
Hunters, with loud 'Halloo,' sight of their prey do hail,
Loudly they chide the fox, nor scolding speech doth fail,
Threaten him once and oft, and 'thief' they call him there—
The hounds are on his trail, tarry he may not dare,
Oft would they him out-run, and head him ere he passed,
Double again he must – wily the fox, and fast,
Thus, by his skill he led master and huntsmen bold

O'er hill, o'er dale, by mount, by woodland, and by
  wold;
While the good knight at home doth soundly sleep, I
  ween,
All comely curtained round, on morning cold and keen.
But Love the lady fair had suffered not to sleep,
That purpose to impair which she in heart doth keep.
Quickly she rose her up, and thither took her way
In mantle meet enwrapped, which swept the ground
  alway.
Within, 't was finely furred, and bordered with the
  same,
No gold doth bind her head but precious stones,
  aflame,
Within her tresses wound, by twenties cluster fair;
Her face, and eke her throat, the mantle leaveth bare,
Bare is her snow-white breast, and bare her back to
  sight;
Passing the chamber door, she shuts it close and
  tight—
Setting the window wide, she calls her knight alway,
And, laughing, chideth him in merry words and gay,
  With cheer,
   'Ah, man! Why dost thou sleep?
   The morn dawns fair and clear,'
   Gawain, in slumber deep,
   Dreaming, her voice did hear.

XXV

Drowsing, he dreamed, the knight, a dream with
  travail fraught,
As men, in morning hours, are plagued with troubled
  thought;

How destiny, next morn, his weird should duly dight,
When, at the Chapel Green, he needs must meet that
  knight,
And there his buffet bide, nor make there for debate—
But, came that comely dame, his wits he summoned
  straight,
Aroused him from his sleep, and spake full speedily;
That lady drew anigh, sweet was her smile to see—
She bent her o'er his face, and kissed him, fair and
  free.
A greeting fit he gave, in words of gladsome cheer,
So glorious her guise, clad in such goodly gear,
Her features faultless all, her colour fair and fine,
The springs of joy well free, warming his heart like
  wine;
Their seemly smiles full swift were smitten into mirth,
Bliss, and good fellowship, betwixt the twain to birth
  did win—
    Their words were fair and good,
    Weal reigned those walls within,
    Yet peril 'twixt them stood,
    Nor might she nearer win.

XXVI

She pressed that prince of price so close, I trow, that
  day,
Leaning so nigh her point, that need upon him lay
To take her proffered love, or roughly say her nay—
For courtesy his care, lest he be craven knight,
And more, lest mischief fall, in that he sin outright,
And thus betray his host, the lord of house and hall,
'God shield me,' quoth the knight, 'that e'er such
  chance befall!'

Forthwith, with laughter light, he strove to lay aside
All speech of special grace her lips might speak that
  tide;
Then quoth she to the knight: 'I hold ye worthy blame
An ye love not that life which here your love doth
  claim,
And lieth wounded here, above all else on earth,
Save ye a true love have ye hold of better worth,
And to that lady fair your faith so fast ye hold,
Ye may not list my words – Save ye that tale have told
That will I not believe – I pray ye, of a sooth,
For all the love on life, hide not from me the truth
  for guile?'
    The knight quoth: 'By Saint John,
    (And gaily did he smile)
    Of true love have I none,
    Nor will I, for a while!'

XXVII

'That word,' the lady quoth, 'methinks hath grieved
  me more,
Yet I my answer take, altho' I sorrow sore;
But kiss me kindly now, ere yet I go my way
My fate to mourn on mould, as she who loveth may.'
Sighing, she swayed adown, and kissed the knight so
  good,
Then raised her up again, and spake e'en as she stood:
'At this our parting, dear, grant me this grace for love,
Give me somewhat as gift, if it be but thy glove,
That I may think on thee, and so my grief may still
'Now, I wis,' quoth the knight, 'I would I had at will,
The thing I hold on earth most precious, it were thine,
Ye have deserved, I trow, by friendship fair and fine,

SIR GAWAIN AND THE GREEN KNIGHT

A guerdon goodlier far than I might e'er bestow!
But here, by gift of love, small profit might ye know,
Nor were ye honoured now, had ye at this time aught
Or glove, or other gift, from Gawain, as ye sought;
Here thro' the land I fare on errand strange and dread,
No men have I with mails, or trinkets, at this stead,
That much misliketh me, lady, for this thy sake,
Yet, be 't for good or ill, each man his chance must take
  aright—'
    'Thou knight of honour, nay'
    (So spake the lady bright),
    'Tho' no gift be my pay
    Somewhat I'll give my knight.'

XXVIII

She proffered him a ring, of red gold fashioned fair,
A sparkling stone, I trow, aloft the setting bare,
Its gleam, in sooth, outshone the sunlight's ruddy ray,
I wot well that its worth no man might lightly pay.
Gawain the ring refused, and readily he spake:
'No gift, my lady gay, of goodwill will I take,
Since I have naught to give naught will I take of thee—'
Straitly she prayed, Gawain refused her steadfastly,
Sware swiftly on his sooth, that ring he would not take—
The lady, sorely grieved, in this wise further spake:
'An ye refuse my ring, methinks, the cause shall be
Ye deem ye were too much beholden unto me,
I'll here my girdle give as lesser gift this tide—'
She loosed a silken lace that hung low at her side,
Upon her kirtle knit, beneath her mantle's fold,

TRANSLATED BY JESSIE WESTON

With green silk was it gay, entwined with threads of gold,
Braided in cunning wise, by skilful fingers wrought;
She proffered it the knight, and blithely him besought
To take this as her gift, tho' worthless all it were—
But still he said her nay, and, ever steadfast, sware
He would nor gift nor gold, ere God would give him grace
Well to achieve the chance t'wards which he set his face—
'Therefore, I pray ye now, be not displeased at this,
But let the matter be, I may not grant, I wis,
   thy prayer
     Much do I owe to thee
     For this, thy gentle care,
     By heat, by cold, I'll be
     Thy servant everywhere.'

XXIX

'Do ye refuse this silk,' so quoth the gentle dame,
'For its simplicity? I grant ye of that same;
Lo! light it is to hold, and less its cost, I ween,
Yet who the virtue knew that knit therein hath been,
Would peradventure prize it higher for its grace—
Whoso shall gird himself with this same woven lace
The while 't is knotted well around him, 't is a charm,
And no man upon mould may wreak him hurt or harm,
And ne'er may he be slain by magic, or by spell—'
Sir Gawain, in his heart, that hour bethought him well,
That lace a jewel were against the jeopardy
Which, at the Chapel Green, did wait him presently,

Might he escape un-slain, the sleight he deemed were good;
Thus suffered he her prayer, and shewed a gentler mood.
She pressed on him her gift, and urged him loud and still,
He granted her the grace, she gave it of good will,
And, for her sake, besought he tell the matter ne'er,
But hide it from her lord, he sware it fast and fair,
That no man, save them twain, should this, their secret, share
for naught—
    He thanked her oft, I wis,
    joyful of heart and thought,
    Her true knight did she kiss
    Thrice, ere she leave besought.

XXX

Then, laughing, saith, 'Farewell,' and from the room doth go
For more mirth of that man, I wot, she may not know;
When she hath gone, Gawain doth from his couch arise,
And swiftly robes himself in rich and royal wise,
Taketh the love-lace green, his lady's gift so fair,
That wound around his waist he doth well hidden bear.
Then to the chapel, swift, the knight doth take his way,
And, seeking out a priest, he privily doth pray
He may his life unfold, that he may better know
How his soul may be saved, when he from hence shall go.

TRANSLATED BY JESSIE WESTON

Shrived was he surely there – he shewed his misdeeds all,
Or less they be or more, and did for mercy call,
Then, from the listening priest, doth absolution pray—
Assoiléd well he was, and set as clean alway
As if the morrow's morn the day of doom should be.
Sithen he makes good cheer amid the ladies free,
With comely carols there, all joys men may devise,
(As ne'er before that day, methinks, had been his wise)
with bliss—
 That all men marvelled there
 And said of him, I wis,
 Such semblance gay he ware
 As none had seen ere this.

XXXI

Now let him linger there where love his share shall be—
The lord is yet afield, leading his folk so free,
Now hath he slain the fox, that he hath chased all day—
As he thro' spinney sped, eager to spy his prey,
There, where he heard the hounds that close on his track lay,
Lo! Reynard, running low, thro' tangled grove he steals,
And all the yelping pack of hounds are at his heels.
The knight, he saw the beast, and would his coming wait,
Drew forth his brand so bright, and flung it swift and straight,
The fox, the sharp sword shunned, to swerve aside was fain,

A hound doth hold him fast ere he might turn again,
Beneath the horse's feet the pack upon him fell,
Worried their wily prey with many a yap and yell,
The lord, he lights adown, the fox he seizes there,
Swiftly he snatches him from out the jaws that tear,
Holding him high o'er head, he halloos loud and gay,
While many a gallant hound doth round him spring
    and bay.
Thither the huntsmen hie, their horns sound merrily,
Answering each to each, till all their master see.
That noble company, they gather fair and fast,
All who the bugle bare together blew a blast,
While they who had no horn, they halloo'd loud and
    clear;
It was the merriest meet that ever man might hear
The clamour that was raised o'er Reynard's doom so
    drear
    Then, gay,
        The hounds they there reward,
        Rubbing their heads that day—
        Now have they ta'en Reynard
        And stript his pelt away.

XXXII

And then they hied them home, for night-fall was full
    nigh,
Blowing a shattering blast on horn, with notes so high,
The lord at last alights before his home so dear,
A fire he finds on floor – his guest, he sitteth near,
Gawain the good, who glad and joyous was withal,
For, mid the ladies fair, bliss to his lot did fall.
He ware a robe of blue, e'en to the earth it fell,
His surcoat, softly furred, became him passing well;

Of self-same stuff, the hood upon his shoulders lay,
Bordered and bound the twain with fur alike that day.
His host he met forthwith, there, in the midmost hall,
A goodly greeting gave, and joyful spake withal;
'Now shall I first fulfil thy forward, mine and thine,
Which we together sware whenas ye spared no wine.'
With that he clasped the knight, and gave him kisses three,
Setting them on his lips with all solemnity.
'By Christ,' then quoth the host: 'good fortune yours hath been,
If for such chance ye gave a fair exchange, I ween!'
'Thereof small need to speak—' the hero straightway said,
'Since light the cost, and swift, methinks, the price I paid.'
'By Mary,' quoth his host, 'in that am I behind,
I hunted all this day, and yet I naught might find
Save this foul fox's pelt, fiend take the thing alway,
Methinks for precious gifts the same were sorry pay.
And ye have rendered me three kisses here to-day
  right good—'
    'Enough,' quoth Sir Gawain,
    'I thank ye, by the Rood.'
    Then how the fox was slain
    He told him as they stood.

XXXIII

Of mirth, of minstrelsy, of meat, they take their fill,
And make them merry there, as men may do at will,
With ladies' laughter light, and many a merry jest,
So joyful were the twain, the host, and his good guest,
E'en as they drunken were, or e'en had waxen fey—

SIR GAWAIN AND THE GREEN KNIGHT

The lord, and e'en his men made many a jest so gay,
Until at length the time for severance was o'er past,
Each baron to his bed betook him at the last.
Then first, Sir Gawain good, leave of his host would
    pray
Thanking him fair and free, and thus he spake alway:
'For this fair sojourning your honour be increased,
The High King grant ye this, I pray, at this high feast.
Your servant here am I, an so your will may be—
With morn I needs must fare, e'en as I told to ye,
A guide ye promised sure, to shew to me the way
To that same Chapel Green, where, on the New Year's
    Day
With God's will shall be dealt my doom, and this, my
    weird—'
'In good faith,' quoth the host, 'be not for that afeard,
Of good will shall I give all that to ye I hight—'
A servant then he called, to shew the way aright
Fair o'er the downs, that so Gawain should have no
    need
To wend by words, but through the copse, might make
    with speed
        his way—
    For gracious fare, Gawain,
    With gracious words would pay,
    And from the ladies twain
    His leave was loth to pray.

XXXIV

Careful he kissed the twain, and spake them both full
    fair,
Well may they thrive for thanks he presseth on them
    there.

And in the selfsame wise those ladies make reply,
Commending him to Christ, with many a piteous sigh.
Then from the household all, in courteous wise he 'ld part,
And each man that he met, he thanked him from his heart
For service, solace fair, and for the pains they knew
In that they busied them to do him service true.
And all to say 'Farewell,' I trow, such sorrow felt
As if in worthy wise long years with him they 'd dwelt.
With torches burning bright, they to his chamber led,
And, that he well might rest, blithely brought him to bed.
But that he soundly slept, in sooth, I dare not say,
Matter enow had he, that came with dawning day
   for thought—
     Now let him lie there still,
     He nigheth what he sought—
     If hearken me ye will
     I'll tell ye how they wrought.

Book IV

I

Now nigheth the New Year, past are the hours of
  night,
And, e'en as God doth will, darkness must yield to
  light,
But weather wild awakes e'en with the New Year's
  birth,
Aloft, the driving clouds cast the keen cold to earth,
Enow of North therein the naked wight to slay—
The snow, it smartly drave across the fells that day,
With whistling blast the wind doth whirl it from on
  high,
Till, in each dale, the drifts both wide and deep they
  lie.
The knight, he hearkened well, as in his bed he lay,
But, tho' his eyes were shut, little he slept alway.
By every cock that crew, the hour right well he knew,
And lightly gat him up, ere yet to dawn it drew,
For in the chamber burned a lamp that gave him light

His chamberlain he called, who answered him forthright,
Bade him his byrnie bring, and saddle his good steed;
The other gat him up, and swiftly fetched his weed,
Then was Sir Gawain clad in fitting wise, and fair,
First, in his clothes he's wrapt, the cold from him to 'ware,
Then he his harness doffs, that well was kept, I ween,
The plates, the coat of mail, alike are polished clean,
And of his byrnie rich, the rings from rust are freed,
'T was fresh as at the first – Of thanks, he fain full meed
   would bring—
   He did on him each piece,
   They lacked no burnishing,
   Gayest from here to Greece,
   His steed he bade them bring.

II

The while in richest weed he doth himself array,
His coat, with cognizance embroidered clear and gay,
On velvet, rich adorned, with stones of virtue high
Well wrought and bound, the seams embroidered cunningly,
And all, with fairest skins, within well furred and lined—
The lace, the lady's gift, he doth not leave behind,
Gawain forgat it not, since 't was for his own good—
He belted fast his brand around him as he stood,
Then twined the token twice, and drew it round him tight,
Well did that silken cord enswathe the goodly knight;
The girdle of green silk, in sooth, beseemed him well,

SIR GAWAIN AND THE GREEN KNIGHT

On cloth of royal red, its hues, they richly tell.
But for that girdle's grace he ware it not, the knight,
Nor for the pendants' pride, tho' polished they, and
   bright,
Nor for the glittering gold, whose gleam the ends doth
   light—
But 't was to save himself, when he must shortly stand
And bide without debate, from knife or glittering
   brand
   a blow—
      Now, armed, the goodly knight
      Forth from the hall doth go,
      On all who there be dight
      His thanks he would bestow.

III

Ready was Gringalet, his charger great and tall,
Stabled the steed had been in fitting wise withal,
Eager to start, the horse delay might little brook—
The knight, he drew anear, and on his coat did look,
Spake softly to himself, and by his sooth he sware,
'The men within this moat for honour fitly care,
May they, with their good lord, all joy henceforward
   share,
And may love be her meed thro' life, that fair ladie,
Who thus a passing guest cherish for charitie,
And honour hold in hand – may He repay withal
Who rules on high, the folk within this goodly hall,
If I my life on land might somewhat longer lead
Then readily reward I'ld give, as fits your meed
He to the stirrup steps, and doth his steed bestride,
Upon his shoulder lays his shield as fit, that tide,
Then spurreth Gringalet, anon, with spurs of gold,

The steed no longer stands, but on the stones so cold
   doth dance—
   Mounted, his squire doth bear
   Aloft, his spear and lance,—
   'Christ keep this castle fair
   And give it aye good chance.'

IV

They let the bridge adown, the gateway, broad and
   wide,
Unbar, and open set the door on either side;
The knight, he crossed himself, and passed the castle
   bound,
Praising the porter good, who, kneeling low on
   ground,
Gave him Good-day, and prayed that God might save
   Gawain—
So doth he wend his way, with one wight in his train,
To lead him to that place of peril stern and grim,
Where he must pay the price, where bale awaiteth
   him.
By hedgerow winds their way, where boughs are
   stripped and bare,
Anon, they climb the cliffs, where cold and chill the
   air,
The heaven its showers up-held, but here on earth 't
   was ill,
In mist was merged the moor, mist clung to every hill,
Each ware a cap of cloud, and cloak of mist so dank;
Bubbling, the brooks they brake in foam upon the
   bank,
Splashed sheer upon the shores, there, where they
   shelved adown,

Yea, lone and drear the way, beneath the dark wood's
   frown
Until the rising sun with gold the hillcrest crown
   that tide—
   They climbed a hill full high
   White snow lay on its side,
   The guide, who rode hard by,
   Now bade him to abide.

V

'Now lord, as I was pledged, I have ye hither led,
Now are ye nigh the place of note, your quest is sped
That ye have straitly sought, and asked for specially,
But now I know ye well, in sooth, I'ld say to ye—
(Since ye be such a lord that men full well may love,)
Would ye but work my will your welfare it might
   prove
The place whereto ye pass right perilous men hold,
A wight doth ward that waste, the worst is he on
   mould,
For stiff is he, and stern, and over keen to strike,
For height on middle-earth no man hath seen his like;
Bigger of body he, than any four who won
A place in Arthur's house, yea, e'en were Hector one!
And this his custom cursed – here at the Chapel
   Green
There passeth never man, tho' proud in arms, I ween,
But he doth do to death by dint of deadly blow,
For all discourteous he, nor mercy doth he know.
Chaplain be he, or churl, who by that chapel rides,
Mass priest, or hooded monk, or any man beside,
Is he as fain to slay as he himself to live—
So soothly as ye sit on steed, this rede I give:

TRANSLATED BY JESSIE WESTON

Go ye there, with his will, ye come not hence alive—
Trow me, I speak the truth – yea, had ye twenty lives to spend—
    Long time hath he dwelt here,
    His conquests know no end,
    Against his dints so drear
    No shield may ye defend.

VI

'Wherefore, Sir Gawain good, let ye this man alone,
And for God's sake, I pray, from this place get ye gone.
Ride by some other road, Christ speed ye on your way—
I'll hie me home again, but this I'll do alway,
I'll take an oath by God, and all the saints that be,
Or by such hallows all as shall seem best to ye,
That I will hold my peace, and never tell the tale
That ye to face your foe one time for fear did fail.'
'Gramercy,' quoth Gawain (in sooth ill-pleased was he)
'All good may he receive who wisheth good to me,
That thou would'st silence keep, I well believe of thee,
But, tried be thou, and true, if I should turn me here,
And this thy counsel take, and fly for very fear,
I were a coward knight, excused I might not be,
But at the Chapel Green I'll chance it verily,
With that same man I'll speak, e'en as shall please me well
Be it for weal or woe, as fate the lot may tell—
    The knave
    May well be stern in fight,
    Cunning with sword and stave,
    Yet God hath mickle might
    His servant true to save!'

SIR GAWAIN AND THE GREEN KNIGHT

VII

'By Mary,' quoth the squire, 'now ye so much have said
That this, your harm, henceforth, to your own count be laid;
Since ye will lose your life I'll hinder not, nor let,
Take ye your spear in hand, on head the helmet set,
And ride adown this road, that by yon rock doth wind,
Till ye the lowest depth of yonder valley find;
A little to the left, on a lawn, shall ye see,
Within that dreary dale, the chapel, verily,
And him, that grisly giant, who shall its keeper be!
Now may God keep ye well, Sir Gawain, noble knight,
For all the gold on earth, I would not, an I might,
In fellowship with ye but one foot further go—'
With that the squire, he turned his horse's head, and so
He spurred him with his heel, and listed not to spare,
But sprang across the lawn, and left the hero there alone—
 'By God,' thus quoth Gawain,
 I'll neither greet nor groan,
 To God's will am I fain,
 To Him my need is known!'

VIII

He spurreth Gringalet, and down the path doth ride,
Close 'neath a shelving bank, a grove was at his side;
He rides the rough road through, right down into the dale,
Then draweth rein awhile, full wild he deemed that vale;

TRANSLATED BY JESSIE WESTON

No sign of dwelling-place he see'th anywhere,
On either side the banks rise steeply, bleak and bare,
And rough and rugged rocks, with many a stony peak,
That shuddering shadows cast – the place was ill to seek.
Gawain, he stayed his steed, and cast his glance around,
And changed full oft his cheer, ere he that chapel found.
Nor here 't was seen, nor there, right strange the chance he thought;
But soon, upon a lawn, a lawe his eye hath caught,
A smooth hill by a bank, set close beside a burn,
Where by a ford, the flood, forking, aside doth turn,
E'en as they boiled, within, bubbling, the waters spring—
The knight, he turned the rein, his horse to halt doth bring,
At the lawe lights adown, and to a linden bough
The rein, and his good steed, he maketh fast enow.
Then hies him to the hill, and, walking round about,
He cons what it might be, thereof was he in doubt.
A hole was at the end, and one on either side,
And all with grass o'er-grown, in clumps its form that hide,
'T was hollow all within, e'en as a cavern old,
Or crevice of a crag – nor might its use be told right well—
    'Good Lord,' quoth the good knight,
    'Be this the Green Chapel?
    The devil at midnight
    Might here his matins tell!'

IX

'I wis,' so quoth Gawain, 'that wizardry be here,
'T were ill for prayer this place, o'er grown with grasses sere,
'T were fitting, did that wight who wraps himself in green
Do his devotions here in devil's wise, I ween!
By my five wits I feel 't is the foul fiend, in truth,
Who here hath given me tryst, my life he seeks, forsooth!
A chapel of mischance, ill fortune may it win,
'T is the most curséd kirk I e'er set foot within!'
His helmet on his head, his lance gripped fast in hand,
He nighs the rock wherein the dwelling rough doth stand;
Then, from the hill on high, as 't were from out a rock,
On bank beyond the brook, a noise his senses shock;
It clatters thro' the cliffs, as they would cleave in twain,
As one to sharpen scythe on grinding-stone were fain.
Lo! it doth whet and whir as water thro' a mill,
Lo! it doth rush and ring – to hear it was right ill!
Then, 'By God,' quoth Gawain, 'I trow that weapon sheer
They sharpen for that knight who bade me meet him here
this stound.
    Let God work as He will,
    No help elsewhere were found;
    Tho' life be forfeit, still
    I blench not for a sound.'

TRANSLATED BY JESSIE WESTON

X

With that the goodly knight, he called with voice so bold,
'Who waiteth in this place a tryst with me to hold?
For here is Gawain come, here hath he found his way,
If any wight will win aught, let him come to-day,
Or now, or never, so his need be fitly sped—'
A voice spake from the bank, on high, above his head,
'Stay, and I swift will give that which I promised thee—'
Awhile the clamour rang, still rushing rapidly,
The whetstone whirled awhile, ere he his foe might see,
And then, beneath a crag, forth from a cave he sprung,
And, coming from that hole, a weapon round him swung,
A Danish axe, new dight, wherewith the blow to deal,
Bound to the handle fast was the bright blade of steel,
Four foot long, fitly filed, no less, that blade of might,
And all was wrapped and bound with lace that gleamed full bright;
E'en as before was he in gear of green, that knight—
Green was he face and foot, his hair, his beard's full flow,
But this time on the ground that knight afoot doth go,
Stalking, he held the axe, steel downward, at his side,
Thus to the water wins, and takes it in his stride.
He wades not, with his axe he leaps that water's flow,
And fierce, and bold, bestrides the bent, all white with snow
    that day—
        Sir Gawain met the knight,
        No greeting did he pay,
        The other quoth: 'Aright
        Hast thou kept tryst to-day!'

XI

'Gawain,' quoth the Green Knight, 'now may God give thee grace,
Welcome art thou, I wis, to this, my dwelling-place;
Thy travel hast thou timed e'en as true man should do—
Thou know'st the forward fast we sware betwixt us two;
This day, a twelve-month past, thy share thereof didst take,
And I, at this New Year, should fitting answer make.
Here in this dale alone, I trow, we be to-day,
To deal as likes us best, with none to say us nay;
Now doff thy helm from head, thy payment forthwith take,
And with no more debate than I with thee did make
When thou whipped off my head, with but one sweeping blow—'
'Nay, by God,' quoth Gawain, 'to whom my life I owe,
Nor greet will I, nor groan, for grief that may befall,
Deal, an thou wilt, the stroke, still will I stand, withal,
Nor bandy words with thee, nor e'er for mercy call—'
    Straight there
        He bent adown his head,
        And shewed his neck all bare,
        No sign he gave of dread,
        But made as free from care.

XII

Then swift the knight in green made ready for the fray,
And gripped his grim tool fast, as fain Gawain to slay,

TRANSLATED BY JESSIE WESTON

With all his body's force the axe aloft he bare,
A mighty feint he made to deal a death-blow there,
Yea, had he driven adown in wise as he made show
That valiant knight had died beneath the deadly blow.
But as the gisarme fell Gawain, he swerved aside,
E'en as, with fell intent, it did toward him glide;
His shoulders shrank before the sharply gleaming blade,.
The other, as he flinched, the axe from falling stayed—
He doth reprove that prince in proud and scornful
   mood:
'Thou art not that Gawain whom men aye deem so
   good,
Who never waxed afraid, by mountain, or by vale,
Now, ere thou feelest hurt, for fear thine heart doth
   fail—
Such cowardice in such knight I never thought to
   know—
I never flinched nor fled, when thou didst aim thy
   blow,
I made no parleying there, within King Arthur's hall,
My head rolled to my feet, I shewed no fear withal;
And thou, ere harm be done, full sore afraid dost seem—
Henceforward, of us twain the braver men shall deem
   me aye—'
     'I shrank once,' quoth Gawain,
     'Henceforth thy stroke I'll stay,
     Tho' none may set again
     The head that falls to-day!'

XIII

'But haste thee, man, I' faith, thy task to end to bring,
Deal me my destiny, make no more dallying,
For I will stand thy stroke, and start no more, I trow,

SIR GAWAIN AND THE GREEN KNIGHT

Till thine axe hitteth me – my word be gage enow!'
'Have at thee!' quoth the knight, and with his axe made play
With wrathful mien and grim, as mad he were alway.
He struck a mighty blow, yet never wound he dealt,
The axe, his hand withheld, ere Gawain harm had felt.
The knight that stroke abode, nor flinched, that hero free,
But stood still as a stone, or stump of ancient tree
That rooted in the ground with hundred roots hath been—
Right gaily then he quoth, the giant garbed in green,
'So, now thine heart is whole, the stroke I'll deal this tide,
Thine hood, that Arthur gave, I prithee hold aside,
And keep thy neck thus bent, that naught may o'er it fall—'
Gawain was greatly wroth, and grimly spake withal:
'Why talk on thus, Sir Knight? o'er-long thy threats so bold,
I trow me in thine heart misgivings thou dost hold!'
'Forsooth,' quoth the Green Knight, 'since fierce thy speech alway
I will no longer let thine errand wait its pay
 but strike
    He frowned with lip and brow,
    Made feint as he would strike
    Who hopes no aid, I trow,
    May well such pass mislike.

XIV

Lightly he lifts the axe, and lo! it falleth fair,
The sharp blade somewhat bit into the neck so bare;

But, tho' he swiftly struck, he hurt him no whit more
Save only on that side where thro' the skin it shore;
E'en to the flesh, I trow, it cut, the blade so good,
And o'er his shoulders ran to earth the crimson blood.
Sir Gawain saw his blood gleam red on the white snow
And swift he sprang aside, more than a spear-length's throw;
With speed his helmet good upon his head set fast,
His trusty shield and true, he o'er his shoulders cast,
Drew forth his brand so bright, and fiercely spake alway:
(I trow that in this world he ne'er was half so gay
Since first, from mother's womb he saw the light of day—)
'Now man, withhold thy blow, and proffer me no more,
A stroke here from thy hand without dispute I bore,
Would'st thou another give, that same I'll here repay,
Give thee as good again, thereto have tryst to-day,
and now—
    But one stroke to me falls,
    So ran the oath, I trow,
    We sware in Arthur's halls,
    And therefore guard thee now!'

XV

The Green Knight drew aback, and on his axe did lean,
Setting the shaft to ground, upon the blade so keen,
He looked upon the knight awhile, there, on the land,
Doughty, and void of dread, dauntless doth Gawain stand,
All armed for strife – at heart it pleased him mightily,

Then, with voice loud and clear he speaketh merrily,
Hailing aloud the knight, gaily to him doth say:
'Bold Sir, upon this bent be not so stern to-day,
For none, discourteous, here methinks mishandled thee,
Nor will, save e'en as framed at court in forward free;
I promised thee a stroke, thou hast it at this same,
With that be thou content, I make no further claim.
An such had been my will, a buffet, verily,
Rougher I might have dealt, and so done worse to thee,
Firstly, I menace made with but a feignéd blow,
And harmed thee ne'er a whit; that, I would have thee know,
Was for the forward fast we made in that first night
When thou didst swear me troth, and kept that troth aright,
Thou gav'st me all thy gain, e'en as good knight and true—
Thus for the morrow's morn another feint was due,
Didst kiss my gentle wife, and kisses gave again—
For these two from mine axe two blows I did but feign this stead—

    To true man payment true,
    Of that may none have dread,
    Then, didst withhold my due,
    Therefore thy blood I shed.'

XVI

"'T is my weed thou dost wear, that self-same lace of green,
'T was woven by my wife, I know it well, I ween,
Thy kisses all I know, thy ways, thy virtues all,

The wooing of my wife, 't was I who willed it all;
I bade her test thy truth – By God who gave me birth
Thou art the truest knight that ever trode this earth!
As one a pearl doth prize, measured 'gainst pease, tho' white,
So do I hold Gawain above all other knight!
Didst thou a little lack, Sir Knight, in loyalty,
'T was not for woman's love, or aught of villainy,
'T was but for love of life, therefore I blame thee less—'
Awhile Sir Gawain stood, silent, for sorriness,
Right sore aggrieved was he, and angered at that same;
Then all his body's blood rushed to his face in flame,
And all for shame he shrank, while yet the Green Knight spake—
Then in this fashion first lament the knight did make;
'Covetousness, accurst be thou, and cowardice,
In virtue's stead ye bring both villainy and vice—'
With that he caught the knot, and loosed the lace so bright,
Giveth the girdle green again to the Green Knight,
'Lo! there the false thing take, a foul fate it befall,
Fear of thy blow, it taught me cowardice withal,
With custom covetous to league me, and thus wrong
Largesse and loyalty, which do to knights belong.
Faulty am I, and false, to fear hath been a prey.
From treachery and untruth is sorrow born alway,
   and care—
      So here I own to thee
      That faithless did I fare;
      Take thou thy will of me,
      Henceforth I'll be more 'ware!'

XVII

The Green Knight laughed aloud, and spake right merrily,
'Whole am I of the hurt that thou didst deal to me;
Thy misdeeds hast thou shewn, and hast confessed thee clean,
Hast borne the penance sharp of this, mine axe-edge keen,
I hold thee here absolved, and purged as clean this morn
As thou hadst ne'er done wrong since the day thou wert born.
This girdle, hemmed with gold, Sir Knight, I give to thee,
'T is green as this my robe, as thou right well may'st see,
Look thou thereon, Gawain, whenas thou forth dost fare,
Mid many a prince of price, and this for token bear
Of chance midst chivalrous knights, that thou didst here abide—
And thou, in this New Year with me shalt homeward ride,
With me in revel spend the remnant of this tide
    I ween—'
        The lord, he held him fast,
        Quoth: 'Tho' my wife hath been
        Your foe, that is well past,
        Peace be ye twain between!'

TRANSLATED BY JESSIE WESTON

XVIII

'Nay, forsooth,' quoth Gawain, he seized his helm full fain,
And set it on his head, and thanked his host again;
'Sad was my sojourning, yet bliss be yours alway,
May He, who ruleth all, right swiftly ye repay.
To her, your comely wife, commend me courteously,
Yea, and that other dame, honoured they both may be
Who thus their knight with craft right skilful did beguile—
And yet small marvel 't is if one, thro' woman's wile
Befooled shall be oft-times, and brought to sorrow sore,
For so was he betrayed, Adam, our sire, of yore,
And Solomon full oft! Delilah swift did bring
Samson unto his fate; and David too, the king,
By Bathsheba ensnared, grief to his lot must fall—
Since women these beguiled 't were profit great withal
An one might love them well, and yet believe them not!
For of all men on earth had these the fairest lot,
All other they excelled 'neath Heaven – if they, God wot,
   be mused,
      Yielding themselves to wile
      Of women, whom they used,
      Then, an one me beguile,
      I hold me well excused.'

XIX

'But for your girdle, good, may God the gift repay,
I take it of good will; not for its gold alway,

SIR GAWAIN AND THE GREEN KNIGHT

For samite, nor for silk, nor for its pendants fair,
For worship, nor for weal, will I that token wear;
In sign of this, my sin, the silk I still shall see,
And, riding in renown, reproach me bitterly,
Of this my fault, how flesh is all too frail, and fain
To yield when sore enticed, and gather to it stain.
Thus, when for prowess fair in arms I yield to pride,
I 'll look upon this lace, and so more humbly ride.
But one thing would I pray, an so it please ye well,
Lord are ye of this land, where I awhile did dwell
With ye in worship fair – (For this, reward be told
From Him who sits on high, and doth the world uphold–)
But tell me now your name, no more from ye I crave–'
'That truly will I tell,' so spake that baron brave:
'Bernlak de Hautdesert, so men me rightly call—
'T is she, Morgain la Faye, who dwelleth in mine hall,
(Who knoweth many a craft, well versed in cunning wile,
Mistress of Merlin erst,) doth many a man beguile,
(And many a druerie dear she dealt with that same wight,
Who was a skilful clerk, and well he knew each knight of fame–)
    Morgain, the goddess, she,
    So men that lady name,
    And none so proud shall be
    But she his pride can tame!

XX

'She sent me in this guise unto King Arthur's hall
To test your knightly pride, if it were sooth, withal,

The fair renown that runs, of this, your Table Round,
'T was she taught me the craft which ye so strange have found,
To grieve Gaynore, the queen, and her to death to fright
Thro' fear of that same man who spake, a ghastly sight,
Before the table high, with severed head in hand—
'T is she, that ancient dame ye saw in this my land,
And she is e'en thine aunt, sister to Arthur true,
Born of Tintagel's dame, whom later Uther knew,
And gat with her a son, Arthur, our noble king,
Therefore unto thine aunt I would thee straightway bring,
Make merry in mine house, my men are to thee fain,
And I wish thee as well, here on my faith, Gawain,
As any man on earth, for true art thou, and tried—'
But yet he said him 'nay' with him he would not ride.
They clasp, and kiss again – the other, each commends
Unto the Prince of Peace, and there they part as friends
   on mould—
     To the king's hall, I ween,
     Sir Gawain rideth bold,
     He gat, that knight in green,
     Where'er he would on wold.

XXI

The wild ways of the world Sir Gawain now must trace
A-horse, of this his life, he now hath gotten grace;
He harbours oft in house, and oft, I ween, without,
Oft venture bold, in vale, vanquished in battle stout,

Such as, at this same time, I care not to recall—
Whole was the hurt he won upon his neck withal,
And the bright belt of green he ware about him
   wound,
Even in baldric's wise, fast at his side 't was bound;
'Neath his left arm the lace was fastened in a knot,
This token of his fault he bare with him, I wot.
So cometh he to court, all hale, the knight so true,
Weal wakened in those halls whenas the dwellers
   knew
That good Gawain had come – Methinks they deemed
   it gain,
To greet that knight with kiss the king and queen
   were fain,
And many a valiant knight would kiss and clasp him
   there—
Eager, they tidings ask, How did his venture fare
And he doth truly tell of all his toil and care;
Of the Green Chapel's chance, the fashion of the
   knight,
The lady's proffered love, last, of the lace aright
He tells, and on his neck he shews them, as a brand,
The cut that, for his fault, he won from that knight's
   hand
   in blame
      Grieving, he spake alway,
      And groaned for very shame,
      The red blood rose, that day,
      E'en to his face, like flame.

XXII

'Lo! lord,' so spake the knight, handling the lace so
   fair,

TRANSLATED BY JESSIE WESTON

'See here the brand of blame that on my neck I bear,
Lo! here the harm and loss I to myself have wrought,
The cowardice covetous in which I there was caught,
This token of untruth, wherein I was held fast;
And I this needs must wear long as my life shall last.
For none may hide his harm, nor may that be undone,
Once caught within a snare the net is ne'er unspun!'
The king, he cheered the knight, the courtiers, with
   their lord,
Laughed loudly at the tale, and sware with one accord,
That lords and ladies all, of this, the Table Round,
Each of the Brotherhood, should bear, as baldric
   bound,
About his waist, a band, a badge of green so bright,
This would they fitly wear in honour of that knight.
With one accord they sware, those knights so good and
   true,
And he who bare that badge the greater honour knew.
The best book of Romance, in that 't is written all,
How in King Arthur's days this venture did befall,
The Brutus books thereof, I trow, shall witness bear—
And since Brutus the bold at first did hither fare,
Whose fathers the assault and siege of Troy did share,
   I wis,
      Many have been of yore
      The ventures such as this,
      Christ, who a thorn-crown bore,
      Bring us unto His bliss! Amen.

Classic Literature: Words and Phrases
adapted from the Collins English Dictionary

Accoucheur NOUN a male midwife or doctor ❑ *I think my sister must have had some general idea that I was a young offender whom an Accoucheur Policeman had taken up (on my birthday) and delivered over to her* (*Great Expectations* by Charles Dickens)

addled ADJ confused and unable to think properly ❑ *But she counted and counted till she got that addled* (*The Adventures of Huckleberry Finn* by Mark Twain)

admiration NOUN amazement or wonder ❑ *lifting up his hands and eyes by way of admiration* (*Gulliver's Travels* by Jonathan Swift)

afeard ADJ afeard means afraid ❑ *shake it–and don't be afeard* (*The Adventures of Huckleberry Finn* by Mark Twain)

affected VERB affected means to assume the appearance of ❑ *Hadst thou affected sweet divinity* (*Doctor Faustus 5.2* by Christopher Marlowe)

aground ADV when a boat runs aground, it touches the ground in a shallow part of the water and gets stuck ❑ *what kep' you?–boat get aground?* (*The Adventures of Huckleberry Finn* by Mark Twain)

ague NOUN a fever in which the patient has alternate hot and cold shivering fits ❑ *his exposure to the wet and cold had brought on fever and ague* (*Oliver Twist* by Charles Dickens)

alchemy ADJ false or worthless ❑ *all wealth alchemy* (*The Sun Rising* by John Donne)

all alike PHRASE the same all the time ❑ *Love, all alike* (*The Sun Rising* by John Donne)

alow and aloft PHRASE alow means in the lower part or bottom, and aloft means on the top, so alow and aloft means on the top and in the bottom or throughout ❑ *Someone's turned the chest out alow and aloft* (*Treasure Island* by Robert Louis Stevenson)

ambuscade NOUN ambuscade is not a proper word. Tom means an ambush, which is when a group of people attack their enemies, after hiding and waiting for them ❑ *and so we would lie in ambuscade, as he called it* (*The Adventures of Huckleberry Finn* by Mark Twain)

amiable ADJ likeable or pleasant ❑ *Such amiable qualities must speak for themselves* (*Pride and Prejudice* by Jane Austen)

amulet NOUN an amulet is a charm thought to drive away evil spirits. ❑ *uttered phrases at once occult and familiar, like the amulet worn on the heart* (*Silas Marner* by George Eliot)

amusement NOUN here amusement means a strange and disturbing puzzle ❑ *this was an amusement the other way* (*Robinson Crusoe* by Daniel Defoe)

ancient NOUN an ancient was the flag displayed on a ship to show which country it belongs to. It is also called the ensign ❑ *her ancient and pendants out* (*Robinson Crusoe* by Daniel Defoe)

antic ADJ here antic means horrible or grotesque ❑ *armed and dressed after a very antic manner* (*Gulliver's Travels* by Jonathan Swift)

antics NOUN antics is an old word meaning clowns, or people who do silly things to make other people laugh ❑ *And point like antics at his triple crown* (*Doctor Faustus 3.2* by Christopher Marlowe)

appanage NOUN an appanage is a living allowance ❏ *As if loveliness were not the special prerogative of woman—her legitimate appanage and heritage!* (Jane Eyre by Charlotte Brontë)

appended VERB appended means attached or added to ❏ *and these words appended* (Treasure Island by Robert Louis Stevenson)

approver NOUN an approver is someone who gives evidence against someone he used to work with ❏ *Mr. Noah Claypole: receiving a free pardon from the Crown in consequence of being admitted approver against Fagin* (Oliver Twist by Charles Dickens)

areas NOUN the areas is the space, below street level, in front of the basement of a house ❏ *The Dodger had a vicious propensity, too, of pulling the caps from the heads of small boys and tossing them down areas* (Oliver Twist by Charles Dickens)

argument NOUN theme or important idea or subject which runs through a piece of writing ❏ *Thrice needful to the argument which now* (The Prelude by William Wordsworth)

artificially ADV artfully or cleverly ❏ *and he with a sharp flint sharpened very artificially* (Gulliver's Travels by Jonathan Swift)

artist NOUN here artist means a skilled workman ❏ *This man was a most ingenious artist* (Gulliver's Travels by Jonathan Swift)

assizes NOUN assizes were regular court sessions which a visiting judge was in charge of ❏ *you shall hang at the next assizes* (Treasure Island by Robert Louis Stevenson)

attraction NOUN gravitation, or Newton's theory of gravitation ❏ *he predicted the same fate to attraction* (Gulliver's Travels by Jonathan Swift)

aver VERB to aver is to claim something strongly ❏ *for Jem Rodney, the mole catcher, averred that one evening as he was returning homeward* (Silas Marner by George Eliot)

baby NOUN here baby means doll, which is a child's toy that looks like a small person ❏ *and skilful dressing her baby* (Gulliver's Travels by Jonathan Swift)

bagatelle NOUN bagatelle is a game rather like billiards and pool ❏ *Breakfast had been ordered at a pleasant little tavern, a mile or so away upon the rising ground beyond the green; and there was a bagatelle board in the room, in case we should desire to unbend our minds after the solemnity.* (Great Expectations by Charles Dickens)

bah EXCLAM Bah is an exclamation of frustration or anger ❏ *"Bah," said Scrooge.* (A Christmas Carol by Charles Dickens)

bairn NOUN a northern word for child ❏ *Who has taught you those fine words, my bairn?* (Wuthering Heights by Emily Brontë)

bait VERB to bait means to stop on a journey to take refreshment ❏ *So, when they stopped to bait the horse, and ate and drank and enjoyed themselves, I could touch nothing that they touched, but kept my fast unbroken.* (David Copperfield by Charles Dickens)

balustrade NOUN a balustrade is a row of vertical columns that form railings ❏ *but I mean to say you might have got a hearse up that staircase, and taken it broadwise, with the splinter-bar towards the wall, and the door towards the balustrades: and done it easy* (A Christmas Carol by Charles Dickens)

bandbox NOUN a large lightweight box for carrying bonnets or hats ❏ *I am glad I bought my bonnet, if it is only for the fun of having another bandbox* (Pride and Prejudice by Jane Austen)

barren NOUN a barren here is a stretch or expanse of barren land ❏ *a line of upright stones, continued the* *length of the barren* (Wuthering Heights by Emily Brontë)

basin NOUN a basin was a cup without a handle ❏ *who is drinking his tea out of a basin* (Wuthering Heights by Emily Brontë)

battalia NOUN the order of battle ❏ *till I saw part of his army in battalia* (Gulliver's Travels by Jonathan Swift)

battery NOUN a Battery is a fort or a place where guns are positioned ❏ *You bring the lot to me, at that old Battery over yonder* (Great Expectations by Charles Dickens)

battledore and shuttlecock NOUN The game battledore and shuttlecock was an early version of the game now known as badminton. The aim of the early game was simply to keep the shuttlecock from hitting the ground. ❏ *Battledore and shuttlecock's a wery good game vhen you an't the shuttlecock and two lawyers the battledores, in which case it gets too excitin' to be pleasant* (Pickwick Papers by Charles Dickens)

beadle NOUN a beadle was a local official who had power over the poor ❏ *But these impertinences were speedily checked by the evidence of the surgeon, and the testimony of the beadle* (Oliver Twist by Charles Dickens)

bearings NOUN the bearings of a place are the measurements or directions that are used to find or locate it ❏ *the bearings of the island* (Treasure Island by Robert Louis Stevenson)

beaufet NOUN a beaufet was a sideboard ❏ *and sweet-cake from the beaufet* (Emma by Jane Austen)

beck NOUN a beck is a small stream ❏ *a beck which follows the bend of the glen* (Wuthering Heights by Emily Brontë)

bedight VERB decorated ❏ *and bedight with Christmas holly stuck into the top.* (A Christmas Carol by Charles Dickens)

Bedlam NOUN Bedlam was a lunatic asylum in London which had statues carved by Caius Gabriel Cibber at its entrance ❏ *Bedlam, and those carved maniacs at the gates* (The Prelude by William Wordsworth)

beeves NOUN oxen or castrated bulls which are animals used for pulling vehicles or carrying things ❏ *to deliver in every morning six beeves* (Gulliver's Travels by Jonathan Swift)

begot VERB created or caused ❏ *Begot in thee* (On His Mistress by John Donne)

behoof NOUN behoof means benefit ❏ *"Yes, young man," said he, releasing the handle of the article in question, retiring a step or two from my table, and speaking for the behoof of the landlord and waiter at the door* (Great Expectations by Charles Dickens)

berth NOUN a berth is a bed on a boat ❏ *this is the berth for me* (Treasure Island by Robert Louis Stevenson)

bevers NOUN a bever was a snack, or small portion of food, eaten between main meals ❏ *that buys me thirty meals a day and ten bevers* (Doctor Faustus 2.1 by Christopher Marlowe)

bilge water NOUN the bilge is the widest part of a ship's bottom, and the bilge water is the dirty water that collects there ❏ *no gush of bilge-water had turned it to fetid puddle* (Jane Eyre by Charlotte Brontë)

bills NOUN bills is an old term meaning prescription. A prescription is the piece of paper on which your doctor writes an order for medicine and which you give to a chemist to get the medicine ❏ *Are not thy bills hung up as monuments* (Doctor Faustus 1.1 by Christopher Marlowe)

black cap NOUN a judge wore a black cap when he was about to sentence a prisoner to death ❏ *The judge assumed the black cap, and the prisoner still stood with the same air and gesture.* (*Oliver Twist* by Charles Dickens)

boot-jack NOUN a wooden device to help take boots off ❏ *The speaker appeared to throw a boot-jack, or some such article, at the person he addressed* (*Oliver Twist* by Charles Dickens)

booty NOUN booty means treasure or prizes ❏ *would be inclined to give up their booty in payment of the dead man's debts* (*Treasure Island* by Robert Louis Stevenson)

Bow Street runner PHRASE Bow Street runners were the first British police force, set up by the author Henry Fielding in the eighteenth century ❏ *as would have convinced a judge or a Bow Street runner* (*Treasure Island* by Robert Louis Stevenson)

brawn NOUN brawn is a dish of meat which is set in jelly ❏ *Heaped up upon the floor, to form a kind of throne, were turkeys, geese, game, poultry, brawn, great joints of meat, suckling-pigs* (*A Christmas Carol* by Charles Dickens)

bray VERB when a donkey brays, it makes a loud, harsh sound ❏ *and she doesn't bray like a jackass* (*The Adventures of Huckleberry Finn* by Mark Twain)

break VERB in order to train a horse you first have to break it ❏ *"If a high-mettled creature like this," said he, "can't be broken by fair means, she will never be good for anything"* (*Black Beauty* by Anna Sewell)

bullyragging VERB bullyragging is an old word which means bullying. To bullyrag someone is to threaten or force someone to do something they don't want to do ❏ *and a lot of loafers bullyragging him for sport* (*The Adventures of Huckleberry Finn* by Mark Twain)

but PREP except for (this) ❏ *but this, all pleasures fancies be* (*The Good-Morrow* by John Donne)

by hand PHRASE by hand was a common expression of the time meaning that baby had been fed either using a spoon or a bottle rather than by breast-feeding ❏ *My sister, Mrs. Joe Gargery, was more than twenty years older than I, and had established a great reputation with herself . . . because she had bought me up "by hand"* (*Great Expectations* by Charles Dickens)

bye-spots NOUN bye-spots are lonely places ❏ *and bye-spots of tales rich with indigenous produce* (*The Prelude* by William Wordsworth)

calico NOUN calico is plain white fabric made from cotton ❏ *There was two old dirty calico dresses* (*The Adventures of Huckleberry Finn* by Mark Twain)

camp-fever NOUN camp-fever was another word for the disease typhus ❏ *during a severe camp-fever* (*Emma* by Jane Austen)

cant NOUN cant is insincere or empty talk ❏ *"Man," said the Ghost, "if man you be in heart, not adamant, forbear that wicked cant until you have discovered What the surplus is, and Where it is."* (*A Christmas Carol* by Charles Dickens)

canty ADJ canty means lively, full of life ❏ *My mother lived til eighty, a canty dame to the last* (*Wuthering Heights* by Emily Brontë)

canvas VERB to canvas is to discuss ❏ *We think so very differently on this point Mr Knightley, that there can be no use in canvassing it* (*Emma* by Jane Austen)

capital ADJ capital means excellent or extremely good ❏ *for it's capital, so shady, light, and big* (*Little Women* by Louisa May Alcott)

capstan NOUN a capstan is a device used on a ship to lift sails and anchors ❏ *capstans going, ships going out to sea, and unintelligible sea creatures roaring curses over the* bulwarks at respondent lightermen (*Great Expectations* by Charles Dickens)

case-bottle NOUN a square bottle designed to fit with others into a case ❏ *The spirit being set before him in a huge case-bottle, which had originally come out of some ship's locker* (*The Old Curiosity Shop* by Charles Dickens)

casement NOUN casement is a word meaning window. The teacher in Nicholas Nickleby misspells window showing what a bad teacher he is ❏ *W-i-n, win, d-e-r, der, winder, a casement.* (*Nicholas Nickleby* by Charles Dickens)

cataleptic ADJ a cataleptic fit is one in which the victim goes into a trancelike state and remains still for a long time ❏ *It was at this point in their history that Silas's cataleptic fit occurred during the prayer-meeting* (*Silas Marner* by George Eliot)

cauldron NOUN a cauldron is a large cooking pot made of metal ❏ *stirring a large cauldron which seemed to be full of soup* (*Alice's Adventures in Wonderland* by Lewis Carroll)

cephalic ADJ cephalic means to do with the head ❏ *with ink composed of a cephalic tincture* (*Gulliver's Travels* by Jonathan Swift)

chaise and four NOUN a closed four-wheel carriage pulled by four horses ❏ *he came down on Monday in a chaise and four to see the place* (*Pride and Prejudice* by Jane Austen)

chamberlain NOUN the main servant in a household ❏ *In those times a bed was always to be got there at any hour of the night, and the chamberlain, letting me in at his ready wicket, lighted the candle next in order on his shelf* (*Great Expectations* by Charles Dickens)

characters NOUN distinguishing marks ❏ *Impressed upon all forms the characters* (*The Prelude* by William Wordsworth)

chary ADJ cautious ❏ *I should have been chary of discussing my guardian too freely even with her* (*Great Expectations* by Charles Dickens)

cherishes VERB here cherishes means cheers or brightens ❏ *some philosophic song of Truth that cherishes our daily life* (*The Prelude* by William Wordsworth)

chickens' meat PHRASE chickens' meat is an old term which means chickens' feed or food ❏ *I had shook a bag of chickens' meat out in that place* (*Robinson Crusoe* by Daniel Defoe)

chimeras NOUN a chimera is an unrealistic idea or a wish which is unlikely to be fulfilled ❏ *with many other wild impossible chimeras* (*Gulliver's Travels* by Jonathan Swift)

chines NOUN chine is a cut of meat that includes part or all of the backbone of the animal ❏ *and they found hams and chines uncut* (*Silas Marner* by George Eliot)

chits NOUN chits is a slang word which means girls ❏ *I hate affected, niminy-piminy chits!* (*Little Women* by Louisa May Alcott)

chopped VERB chopped means come suddenly or accidentally ❏ *if I had chopped upon them* (*Robinson Crusoe* by Daniel Defoe)

chute NOUN a narrow channel ❏ *One morning about day-break, I found a canoe and crossed over a chute to the main shore* (*The Adventures of Huckleberry Finn* by Mark Twain)

circumspection NOUN careful observation of events and circumstances; caution ❏ *I honour your circumspection* (*Pride and Prejudice* by Jane Austen)

clambered VERB clambered means to climb somewhere with difficulty, usually using your hands and your feet ❏ *he clambered up and down stairs* (*Treasure Island* by Robert Louis Stevenson)

TRANSLATED BY JESSIE WESTON

clime NOUN climate ❑ *no season knows nor clime* (The Sun Rising by John Donne)

clinched VERB clenched ❑ *the tops whereof I could but just reach with my fist clinched* (Gulliver's Travels by Jonathan Swift)

close chair NOUN a close chair is a sedan chair, which is an covered chair which has room for one person. The sedan chair is carried on two poles by two men, one in front and one behind ❑ *persuaded even the Empress herself to let me hold her in her close chair* (Gulliver's Travels by Jonathan Swift)

clown NOUN clown here means peasant or person who lives off the land ❑ *In ancient days by emperor and clown* (Ode to a Nightingale by John Keats)

coalheaver NOUN a coalheaver loaded coal onto ships using a spade ❑ *Good, strong, wholesome medicine, as was given with great success to two Irish labourers and a coalheaver* (Oliver Twist by Charles Dickens)

coal-whippers NOUN men who worked at docks using machines to load coal onto ships ❑ *here, were colliers by the score and score, with the coal-whippers plunging off stages on deck* (Great Expectations by Charles Dickens)

cobweb NOUN a cobweb is the net which a spider makes for catching insects ❑ *the walls and ceilings were all hung round with cobwebs* (Gulliver's Travels by Jonathan Swift)

coddling VERB coddling means to treat someone too kindly or protect them too much ❑ *and I've been coddling the fellow as if I'd been his grand-mother* (Little Women by Louisa May Alcott)

coil NOUN coil means noise or fuss or disturbance ❑ *What a coil is there?* (Doctor Faustus 4.7 by Christopher Marlowe)

collared VERB to collar something is a slang term which means to capture. In this sentence, it means he stole it [the money] ❑ *he collared it* (The Adventures of Huckleberry Finn by Mark Twain)

colling VERB colling is an old word which means to embrace and kiss ❑ *and no clasping and colling at all* (Tess of the D'Urbervilles by Thomas Hardy)

colloquies NOUN colloquy is a formal conversation or dialogue ❑ *Such colloquies have occupied many a pair of pale-faced weavers* (Silas Marner by George Eliot)

comfit NOUN sugar-covered pieces of fruit or nut eaten as sweets ❑ *and pulled out a box of comfits* (Alice's Adventures in Wonderland by Lewis Carroll)

coming out VERB when a girl came out in society it meant she was of marriageable age. In order to "come out" girls were expecting to attend balls and other parties during a season ❑ *The younger girls formed hopes of coming out a year or two sooner than they might otherwise have done* (Pride and Prejudice by Jane Austen)

commit VERB commit means arrest or stop ❑ *Commit the rascals* (Doctor Faustus 4.7 by Christopher Marlowe)

commodious ADJ commodious means convenient ❑ *the most commodious and effectual ways* (Gulliver's Travels by Jonathan Swift)

commons NOUN commons is an old term meaning food shared with others ❑ *his pauper assistants ranged themselves behind him; the gruel was served out; and a long grace was said over the short commons.* (Oliver Twist by Charles Dickens)

complacency NOUN here complacency means a desire to please others. To-day complacency means feeling pleased with oneself without good reason. ❑ *Twas thy power that raised the first complacency in me* (The Prelude by William Wordsworth)

complaisance NOUN complaisance was eagerness to please ❑ *we cannot wonder at his complaisance* (Pride and Prejudice by Jane Austen)

complaisant ADJ complaisant means polite ❑ *extremely cheerful and complaisant to their guest* (Gulliver's Travels by Jonathan Swift)

conning VERB conning means learning by heart ❑ *Or conning more* (The Prelude by William Wordsworth)

consequent NOUN consequence ❑ *as avarice is the necessary consequent of old age* (Gulliver's Travels by Jonathan Swift)

consorts NOUN concerts ❑ *The King, who delighted in music, had frequent consorts at Court* (Gulliver's Travels by Jonathan Swift)

conversible ADJ conversible meant easy to talk to, companionable ❑ *He can be a conversible companion* (Pride and Prejudice by Jane Austen)

copper NOUN a copper is a large pot that can be heated directly over a fire ❑ *He gazed in stupefied astonishment on the small rebel for some seconds, and then clung for support to the copper* (Oliver Twist by Charles Dickens)

copper-stick NOUN a copper-stick is the long piece of wood used to stir washing in the copper (or boiler) which was usually the biggest cooking pot in the house ❑ *It was Christmas Eve, and I had to stir the pudding for next day, with a copper-stick, from seven to eight by the Dutch clock* (Great Expectations by Charles Dickens)

counting-house NOUN a counting-house is a place where accountants work ❑ *Once upon a time–of all the good days in the year, on Christmas Eve–old Scrooge sat busy in his counting-house* (A Christmas Carol by Charles Dickens)

courtier NOUN a courtier is someone who attends the king or queen–a member of the court ❑ *next the ten courtiers;* (Alice's Adventures in Wonderland by Lewis Carroll)

covies NOUN covies were flocks of partridges ❑ *and will save all of the best covies for you* (Pride and Prejudice by Jane Austen)

cowed VERB cowed means frightened or intimidated ❑ *it cowed me more than the pain* (Treasure Island by Robert Louis Stevenson)

cozened VERB cozened means tricked or deceived ❑ *Do you remember, sir, how you cozened me* (Doctor Faustus 4.7 by Christopher Marlowe)

cravats NOUN a cravat is a folded cloth that a man wears wrapped around his neck as a decorative item of clothing ❑ *we'd 'a' slept in our cravats to-night* (The Adventures of Huckleberry Finn by Mark Twain)

crock and dirt PHRASE crock and dirt is an old expression meaning soot and dirt ❑ *and the mare catching cold at the door, and the boy grimed with crock and dirt* (Great Expectations by Charles Dickens)

crockery NOUN here crockery means pottery ❑ *By one of the parrots was a cat made of crockery* (The Adventures of Huckleberry Finn by Mark Twain)

crooked sixpence PHRASE it was considered unlucky to have a bent sixpence ❑ *You've got the beauty, you see, and I've got the luck, so you must keep me by you for your crooked sixpence* (Silas Marner by George Eliot)

croquet NOUN croquet is a traditional English summer game in which players try to hit wooden balls through hoops ❑ *and once she remembered trying to box her own ears for having cheated herself in a game of croquet* (Alice's Adventures in Wonderland by Lewis Carroll)

cross PREP across ❑ *The two great streets, which run cross and divide it into four quarters* (Gulliver's Travels by Jonathan Swift)

culpable ADJ if you are culpable for something it means you are to blame ❑ *deep are the sorrows that spring from false ideas for which no man is culpable.* (*Silas Marner* by George Eliot)

cultured ADJ cultivated ❑ *Nor less when spring had warmed the cultured Vale* (*The Prelude* by William Wordsworth)

cupidity NOUN cupidity is greed ❑ *These people hated me with the hatred of cupidity and disappointment.* (*Great Expectations* by Charles Dickens)

curricle NOUN an open two-wheeled carriage with one seat for the driver and space for a single passenger ❑ *and they saw a lady and a gentleman in a curricle* (*Pride and Prejudice* by Jane Austen)

cynosure NOUN a cynosure is something that strongly attracts attention or admiration ❑ *Then I thought of Eliza and Georgiana; I beheld one the cynosure of a ballroom, the other the inmate of a convent cell* (*Jane Eyre* by Charlotte Brontë)

dalliance NOUN someone's dalliance with something is a brief involvement with it ❑ *nor sporting in the dalliance of love* (*Doctor Faustus Chorus* by Christopher Marlowe)

darkling ADV darkling is an archaic way of saying in the dark ❑ *Darkling I listen* (*Ode on a Nightingale* by John Keats)

delf-case NOUN a sideboard for holding dishes and crockery ❑ *at the pewter dishes and delf-case* (*Wuthering Heights* by Emily Brontë)

determined ■ VERB here determined means ended ❑ *and be out of vogue when that was determined* (*Gulliver's Travels* by Jonathan Swift) ■ VERB determined can mean to have been learned or found out especially by investigation or experience ❑ *All the sensitive feelings it wounded so cruelly, all the shame and misery it kept alive within my breast, became more poignant as I thought of this; and I determined that the life was unendurable* (*David Copperfield* by Charles Dickens)

Deuce NOUN a slang term for the Devil ❑ *Ah, I dare say I did. Deuce take me,* he added suddenly, *I know I did. I find I am not quite unscrewed yet.* (*Great Expectations* by Charles Dickens)

diabolical ADJ diabolical means devilish or evil ❑ *and with a thousand diabolical expressions* (*Treasure Island* by Robert Louis Stevenson)

direction NOUN here direction means address ❑ *Elizabeth was not surprised at it, as Jane had written the direction remarkably ill* (*Pride and Prejudice* by Jane Austen)

discover VERB to make known or announce ❑ *the Emperor would discover the secret while I was out of his power* (*Gulliver's Travels* by Jonathan Swift)

dissemble VERB hide or conceal ❑ *Dissemble nothing* (*On His Mistress* by John Donne)

dissolve VERB dissolve here means to release from life, to die ❑ *Fade far away, dissolve, and quite forget* (*Ode on a Nightingale* by John Keats)

distrain VERB to distrain is to seize the property of someone who is in debt in compensation for the money owed ❑ *for he's threatening to distrain for it* (*Silas Marner* by George Eliot)

Divan NOUN a Divan was originally a Turkish council of state–the name was transferred to the couches they sat on and is used to mean this in English ❑ *Mr Brass applauded this picture very much, and the bed being soft and comfortable, Mr Quilp determined to use it, both as a sleeping place by night and as a kind of Divan by day.* (*The Old Curiosity Shop* by Charles Dickens)

divorcement NOUN separation ❑ *By all pains which want and divorcement* *hath* (*On His Mistress* by John Donne)

dog in the manger, PHRASE this phrase describes someone who prevents you from enjoying something that they themselves have no need for ❑ *You are a dog in the manger, Cathy, and desire no one to be loved but yourself* (*Wuthering Heights* by Emily Brontë)

dolorifuge NOUN dolorifuge is a word which Thomas Hardy invented. It means pain-killer or comfort ❑ *as a species of dolorifuge* (*Tess of the D'Urbervilles* by Thomas Hardy)

dome NOUN building ❑ *that river and that mouldering dome* (*The Prelude* by William Wordsworth)

domestic NOUN here domestic means a person's management of the house ❑ *to give some account of my domestic* (*Gulliver's Travels* by Jonathan Swift)

dunce NOUN a dunce is another word for idiot ❑ *Do you take me for a dunce? Go on?* (*Alice's Adventures in Wonderland* by Lewis Carroll)

Ecod EXCLAM a slang exclamation meaning "oh God!" ❑ *"Ecod," replied Wemmick, shaking his head, "that's not my trade."* (*Great Expectations* by Charles Dickens)

egg-hot NOUN an egg-hot (see also "flip" and "negus") was a hot drink made from beer and eggs, sweetened with nutmeg ❑ *She fainted when she saw me return, and made a little jug of egg-hot afterwards to console us while we talked it over.* (*David Copperfield* by Charles Dickens)

encores NOUN an encore is a short extra performance at the end of a longer one, which the entertainer gives because the audience has enthusiastically asked for it ❑ *we want a little something to answer encores with, anyway* (*The Adventures of Huckleberry Finn* by Mark Twain)

equipage NOUN an elegant and impressive carriage ❑ *and besides, the equipage did not answer to any of their neighbours* (*Pride and Prejudice* by Jane Austen)

exordium NOUN an exordium is the opening part of a speech ❑ *"Now, Handel," as if it were the grave beginning of a portentous business exordium, he had suddenly given up that tone* (*Great Expectations* by Charles Dickens)

expect VERB here expect means to wait for ❑ *to expect his farther commands* (*Gulliver's Travels* by Jonathan Swift)

familiars NOUN familiars means spirits or devils who come to someone when they are called ❑ *I'll turn all the lice about thee into familiars* (*Doctor Faustus 1.4* by Christopher Marlowe)

fantods NOUN a fantod is a person who fidgets or can't stop moving nervously ❑ *It most give me the fantods* (*The Adventures of Huckleberry Finn* by Mark Twain)

farthing NOUN a farthing is an old unit of British currency which was worth a quarter of a penny ❑ *Not a farthing less. A great many back-payments are included in it, I assure you.* (*A Christmas Carol* by Charles Dickens)

farthingale NOUN a hoop worn under a skirt to extend it ❑ *A bell with an old voice–which I dare say in its time had often said to the house, Here is the green farthingale* (*Great Expectations* by Charles Dickens)

favours NOUN here favours is an old word which means ribbons ❑ *A group of humble mourners entered the gate: wearing white favours* (*Oliver Twist* by Charles Dickens)

feigned VERB pretend or pretending ❑ *not my feigned page* (*On His Mistress* by John Donne)

fence ■ NOUN a fence is someone who receives and sells stolen goods ❑ *What are you up to? Ill-treating the boys, you covetous, avaricious, in-sa-ti-a-ble old fence?* (*Oliver Twist* by

fence Charles Dickens ■ NOUN defence or protection ❑ *but honesty hath no fence against superior cunning* (*Gulliver's Travels* by Jonathan Swift)

fess ADJ fess is an old word which means pleased or proud ❑ *You'll be fess enough, my poppet* (*Tess of the D'Urbervilles* by Thomas Hardy)

fettered ADJ fettered means bound in chains or chained ❑ *"You are fettered," said Scrooge, trembling. "Tell me why?"* (*A Christmas Carol* by Charles Dickens)

fidges VERB fidges means fidgets, which is to keep moving your hands slightly because you are nervous or excited ❑ *Look, Jim, how my fingers fidges* (*Treasure Island* by Robert Louis Stevenson)

finger-post NOUN a finger-post is a sign-post showing the direction to different places ❑ *"The gallows," continued Fagin, "the gallows, my dear, is an ugly finger-post, which points out a very short and sharp turning that has stopped many a bold fellow's career on the broad highway."* (*Oliver Twist* by Charles Dickens)

fire-irons NOUN fire-irons are tools kept by the side of the fire to either cook with or look after the fire ❑ *the fire-irons came first* (*Alice's Adventures in Wonderland* by Lewis Carroll)

fire-plug NOUN a fire-plug is another word for a fire hydrant ❑ *The pony looked with great attention into a fire-plug, which was near him, and appeared to be quite absorbed in contemplating it* (*The Old Curiosity Shop* by Charles Dickens)

flank NOUN flank is the side of an animal ❑ *And all her silken flanks with garlands dressed* (*Ode on a Grecian Urn* by John Keats)

flip NOUN a flip is a drink made from warmed ale, sugar, spice and beaten egg ❑ *The events of the day, in combination with the twins, if not with the flip, had made Mrs Micawber hysterical, and she shed tears as she replied* (*David Copperfield* by Charles Dickens)

flit VERB flit means to move quickly ❑ *and if he had meant to flit to Thrushcross Grange* (*Wuthering Heights* by Emily Brontë)

floorcloth NOUN a floorcloth was a hard-wearing piece of canvas used instead of carpet ❑ *This avenging phantom was ordered to be on duty at eight on Tuesday morning in the hall (it was two feet square, as charged for floorcloth)* (*Great Expectations* by Charles Dickens)

fly-driver NOUN a fly-driver is a carriage drawn by a single horse ❑ *The fly-drivers, among whom I inquired next, were equally jocose and equally disrespectful* (*David Copperfield* by Charles Dickens)

fob NOUN a small pocket in which a watch is kept ❑ *"Certain," replied the man, drawing a gold watch from his fob* (*Oliver Twist* by Charles Dickens)

folly NOUN folly means foolishness or stupidity ❑ *the folly of beginning a work* (*Robinson Crusoe* by Daniel Defoe)

fond ADJ fond means foolish ❑ *Fond worldling* (*Doctor Faustus 5.2* by Christopher Marlowe)

fondness NOUN silly or foolish affection ❑ *They have no fondness for their colts or foals* (*Gulliver's Travels* by Jonathan Swift)

for his fancy PHRASE for his fancy means for his liking or as he wanted ❑ *and as I did not obey quick enough for his fancy* (*Treasure Island* by Robert Louis Stevenson)

forlorn ADJ lost or very upset ❑ *you are from that day forlorn* (*Gulliver's Travels* by Jonathan Swift)

foster-sister NOUN a foster-sister was someone brought up by the same nurse or in the same household ❑ *I had been his foster-sister* (*Wuthering Heights* by Emily Brontë)

fox-fire NOUN fox-fire is a weak glow that is given off by decaying, rotten wood ❑ *what we must have was a lot of them rotten chunks that's called fox-fire* (The Adventures of Huckleberry Finn by Mark Twain)

frozen sea PHRASE the Arctic Ocean ❑ *into the frozen sea* (Gulliver's Travels by Jonathan Swift)

gainsay VERB to gainsay something is to say it isn't true or to deny it ❑ *"So she had," cried Scrooge. "You're right. I'll not gainsay it, Spirit. God forbid!"* (A Christmas Carol by Charles Dickens)

gaiters NOUN gaiters were leggings made of a cloth or piece of leather which covered the leg from the knee to the ankle ❑ *Mr Knightley was hard at work upon the lower buttons of his thick leather gaiters* (Emma by Jane Austen)

galluses NOUN galluses is an old spelling of gallows, and here means suspenders. Suspenders are straps worn over someone's shoulders and fastened to their trousers to prevent the trousers falling down ❑ *and home-knit galluses* (The Adventures of Huckleberry Finn by Mark Twain)

galoot NOUN a sailor but also a clumsy person ❑ *and maybe a galoot on it chopping* (The Adventures of Huckleberry Finn by Mark Twain)

gayest ADJ gayest means the most lively and bright or merry ❑ *Beth played her gayest march* (Little Women by Louisa May Alcott)

gem NOUN here gem means jewellery ❑ *the mountain shook off turf and flower, had only heath for raiment and crag for gem* (Jane Eyre by Charlotte Brontë)

giddy ADJ giddy means dizzy ❑ *and I wish you wouldn't keep appearing and vanishing so suddenly; you make one quite giddy.* (Alice's Adventures in Wonderland by Lewis Carroll)

gig NOUN a light two-wheeled carriage ❑ *when a gig drove up to the garden gate: out of which there jumped a fat gentleman* (Oliver Twist by Charles Dickens)

gladsome ADJ gladsome is an old word meaning glad or happy ❑ *Nobody ever stopped him in the street to say, with gladsome looks* (A Christmas Carol by Charles Dickens)

glen NOUN a glen is a small valley; the word is used commonly in Scotland ❑ *a beck which follows the bend of the glen* (Wuthering Heights by Emily Brontë)

gravelled VERB gravelled is an old term which means to baffle or defeat someone ❑ *Gravelled the pastors of the German Church* (Doctor Faustus 1.1 by Christopher Marlowe)

grinder NOUN a grinder was a private tutor ❑ *but that when he had had the happiness of marrying Mrs Pocket very early in his life, he had impaired his prospects and taken up the calling of a Grinder* (Great Expectations by Charles Dickens)

gruel NOUN gruel is a thin, watery cornmeal or oatmeal soup ❑ *and the little saucepan of gruel (Scrooge had a cold in his head) upon the hob.* (A Christmas Carol by Charles Dickens)

guinea, half a NOUN half a guinea was ten shillings and sixpence ❑ *but lay out half a guinea at Ford's* (Emma by Jane Austen)

gull VERB gull is an old term which means to fool or deceive someone ❑ *Hush, I'll gull him supernaturally* (Doctor Faustus 3.4 by Christopher Marlowe)

gunnel NOUN the gunnel, or gunwale, is the upper edge of a boat's side ❑ *But he put his foot on the gunnel and rocked her* (The Adventures of Huckleberry Finn by Mark Twain)

gunwale NOUN the side of a ship ❑ *He dipped his hand in the water over the boat's gunwale* (Great Expectations by Charles Dickens)

TRANSLATED BY JESSIE WESTON

Gytrash NOUN a Gytrash is an omen of misfortune to the superstitious, usually taking the form of a hound ❑ *I remembered certain of Bessie's tales, wherein figured a North-of-England spirit, called a "Gytrash"* (*Jane Eyre* by Charlotte Brontë)

hackney-cabriolet NOUN a two-wheeled carriage with four seats for hire and pulled by a horse ❑ *A hackney-cabriolet was in waiting; with the same vehemence which she had exhibited in addressing Oliver, the girl pulled him in with her, and drew the curtains close.* (*Oliver Twist* by Charles Dickens)

hackney-coach NOUN a four-wheeled horse-drawn vehicle for hire ❑ *The twilight was beginning to close in, when Mr Brownlow alighted from a hackney-coach at his own door, and knocked softly.* (*Oliver Twist* by Charles Dickens)

haggler NOUN a haggler is someone who travels from place to place selling small goods and items ❑ *when I be plain Jack Durbeyfield, the haggler* (*Tess of the D'Urbervilles* by Thomas Hardy)

halter NOUN a halter is a rope or strap used to lead an animal or to tie it up ❑ *I had of course long been used to a halter and a headstall* (*Black Beauty* by Anna Sewell)

hamlet NOUN a hamlet is a small village or a group of houses in the countryside ❑ *down from the hamlet* (*Treasure Island* by Robert Louis Stevenson)

hand-barrow NOUN a hand-barrow is a device for carrying heavy objects. It is like a wheelbarrow except that it has handles, rather than wheels, for moving the barrow ❑ *his sea chest following behind him in a hand-barrow* (*Treasure Island* by Robert Louis Stevenson)

handspike NOUN a handspike was a stick which was used as a lever ❑ *a bit of stick like a handspike* (*Treasure Island* by Robert Louis Stevenson)

haply ADV haply means by chance or perhaps ❑ *And haply the Queen-Moon is on her throne* (*Ode on a Nightingale* by John Keats)

harem NOUN the harem was the part of the house where the women lived ❑ *mostly they hang round the harem* (*The Adventures of Huckleberry Finn* by Mark Twain)

hautboys NOUN hautboys are oboes ❑ *sausages and puddings resembling flutes and hautboys* (*Gulliver's Travels* by Jonathan Swift)

hawker NOUN a hawker is someone who sells goods to people as he travels rather than from a fixed place like a shop ❑ *to buy some stockings from a hawker* (*Treasure Island* by Robert Louis Stevenson)

hawser NOUN a hawser is a rope used to tie up or tow a ship or boat ❑ *Again among the tiers of shipping, in and out, avoiding rusty chain-cables, frayed hempen hawsers* (*Great Expectations* by Charles Dickens)

headstall NOUN the headstall is the part of the bridle or halter that goes around a horse's head ❑ *I had of course long been used to a halter and a headstall* (*Black Beauty* by Anna Sewell)

hearken VERB hearken means to listen ❑ *though we sometimes stopped to lay hold of each other and hearken* (*Treasure Island* by Robert Louis Stevenson)

heartless ADJ here heartless means without heart or dejected ❑ *I am not heartless* (*The Prelude* by William Wordsworth)

hebdomadal ADJ hebdomadal means weekly ❑ *It was the hebdomadal treat to which we all looked forward from Sabbath to Sabbath* (*Jane Eyre* by Charlotte Brontë)

highwaymen NOUN highwaymen were people who stopped travellers and robbed them ❑ *We are high-waymen* (*The Adventures of Huckleberry Finn* by Mark Twain)

hinds NOUN hinds means farm hands, or people who work on a farm ❑ *He called his hinds about him* (*Gulliver's Travels* by Jonathan Swift)

histrionic ADJ if you refer to someone's behaviour as histrionic, you are being critical of it because it is dramatic and exaggerated ❑ *But the histrionic muse is the darling* (*The Adventures of Huckleberry Finn* by Mark Twain)

hogs NOUN hogs is another word for pigs ❑ *Tom called the hogs "ingots"* (*The Adventures of Huckleberry Finn* by Mark Twain)

horrors NOUN the horrors are a fit, called delirium tremens, which is caused by drinking too much alcohol ❑ *I'll have the horrors* (*Treasure Island* by Robert Louis Stevenson)

huffy ADJ huffy means to be obviously annoyed or offended about something ❑ *They will feel that more than angry speeches or huffy actions* (*Little Women* by Louisa May Alcott)

hulks NOUN hulks were prison-ships ❑ *The miserable companion of thieves and ruffians, the fallen outcast of low haunts, the associate of the scourings of the jails and hulks* (*Oliver Twist* by Charles Dickens)

humbug NOUN humbug means nonsense or rubbish ❑ *"Bah," said Scrooge. "Humbug!"* (*A Christmas Carol* by Charles Dickens)

humours NOUN it was believed that there were four fluids in the body called humours which decided the temperament of a person depending on how much of each fluid was present ❑ *other peccant humours* (*Gulliver's Travels* by Jonathan Swift)

husbandry NOUN husbandry is farming animals ❑ *bad husbandry were plentifully anointing their wheels* (*Silas Marner* by George Eliot)

huswife NOUN a huswife was a small sewing kit ❑ *but I had put my huswife on it* (*Emma* by Jane Austen)

ideal ADJ ideal in this context means imaginary ❑ *I discovered the yell was not ideal* (*Wuthering Heights* by Emily Brontë)

If our two PHRASE if both our ❑ *If our two loves be one* (*The Good-Morrow* by John Donne)

ignis-fatuus NOUN ignis-fatuus is the light given out by burning marsh gases, which lead careless travellers into danger ❑ *it is madness in all women to let a secret love kindle within them, which, if unreturned and unknown, must devour the life that feeds it; and, if discovered and responded to, must lead ignis-fatuus-like, into miry wilds whence there is no extrication.* (*Jane Eyre* by Charlotte Brontë)

imaginations NOUN here imaginations means schemes or plans ❑ *soon drove out those imaginations* (*Gulliver's Travels* by Jonathan Swift)

impressible ADJ impressible means open or impressionable ❑ *for Marner had one of those impressible, self-doubting natures* (*Silas Marner* by George Eliot)

in good intelligence PHRASE friendly with each other ❑ *that these two persons were in good intelligence with each other* (*Gulliver's Travels* by Jonathan Swift)

inanity NOUN inanity is silliness or dull stupidity ❑ *Do we not wile away moments of inanity* (*Silas Marner* by George Eliot)

incivility NOUN incivility means rudeness or impoliteness ❑ *if it's only for a piece of incivility like to-night's* (*Treasure Island* by Robert Louis Stevenson)

indigenae NOUN indigenae means natives or people from that area ❑ *an exotic that the surly indigenae will not recognise for kin* (*Wuthering Heights* by Emily Brontë)

indocible ADJ unteachable ❑ *so they were the most restive and indocible* (*Gulliver's Travels* by Jonathan Swift)

ingenuity NOUN inventiveness ❑ *entreated me to give him something as an encouragement to ingenuity* (*Gulliver's Travels* by Jonathan Swift)

ingots NOUN an ingot is a lump of a valuable metal like gold, usually shaped like a brick ❑ *Tom called the hogs "ingots"* (*The Adventures of Huckleberry Finn* by Mark Twain)

inkstand NOUN an inkstand is a pot which was put on a desk to contain either ink or pencils and pens ❑ *throwing an inkstand at the Lizard as she spoke* (*Alice's Adventures in Wonderland* by Lewis Carroll)

inordinate ADJ without order. To-day inordinate means "excessive". ❑ *Though yet untutored and inordinate* (*The Prelude* by William Wordsworth)

intellectuals NOUN here intellectuals means the minds (of the workmen) ❑ *those instructions they give being too refined for the intellectuals of their workmen* (*Gulliver's Travels* by Jonathan Swift)

interview NOUN meeting ❑ *By our first strange and fatal interview* (*On His Mistress* by John Donne)

jacks NOUN jacks are rods for turning a spit over a fire ❑ *It was a small bit of pork suspended from the kettle hanger by a string passed through a large door key, in a way known to primitive housekeepers unpossessed of jacks* (*Silas Marner* by George Eliot)

jews-harp NOUN a jews-harp is a small, metal, musical instrument that is played by the mouth ❑ *A jews-harp's plenty good enough for a rat* (*The Adventures of Huckleberry Finn* by Mark Twain)

jorum NOUN a large bowl ❑ *while Miss Skiffins brewed such a jorum of tea, that the pig in the back premises became strongly excited* (*Great Expectations* by Charles Dickens)

jostled VERB jostled means bumped or pushed by someone or some people ❑ *being jostled himself into the kennel* (*Gulliver's Travels* by Jonathan Swift)

keepsake NOUN a keepsake is a gift which reminds someone of an event or of the person who gave it to them. ❑ *books and ornaments they had in their boudoirs at home: keepsakes that different relations had presented to them* (*Jane Eyre* by Charlotte Brontë)

kenned VERB kenned means knew ❑ *though little kenned the lamplighter that he had any company but Christmas!* (*A Christmas Carol* by Charles Dickens)

kennel NOUN kennel means gutter, which is the edge of a road next to the pavement, where rain water collects and flows away ❑ *being jostled himself into the kennel* (*Gulliver's Travels* by Jonathan Swift)

knock-knee ADJ knock-knee means slanted, at an angle. ❑ *LOT 1 was marked in whitewashed knock-knee letters on the brewhouse* (*Great Expectations* by Charles Dickens)

ladylike ADJ to be ladylike is to behave in a polite, dignified and graceful way ❑ *No, winking isn't ladylike* (*Little Women* by Louisa May Alcott)

lapse NOUN flow ❑ *Stealing with silent lapse to join the brook* (*The Prelude* by William Wordsworth)

larry NOUN larry is an old word which means commotion or noisy celebration ❑ *That was all a part of the larry!* (*Tess of the D'Urbervilles* by Thomas Hardy)

laths NOUN laths are strips of wood ❑ *The panels shrunk, the windows cracked; fragments of plaster fell out of the ceiling, and the naked laths were shown instead* (*A Christmas Carol* by Charles Dickens)

leer NOUN a leer is an unpleasant smile ❑ *with a kind of leer* (*Treasure Island* by Robert Louis Stevenson)

lenitives NOUN these are different kinds of drugs or medicines: lenitives and palliatives were pain relievers; aperitives were laxatives; abstersives caused vomiting; corrosives destroyed human tissue; restringents caused constipation; cephalalgics stopped headaches; icterics were used as medicine for jaundice; apophlegmatics were cough medicine, and acoustics were cures for the loss of hearing ❑ *lenitives, aperitives, abstersives, corrosives, restringents, palliatives, laxatives, cephalalgics, icterics, apophlegmatics, acoustics* (Gulliver's Travels by Jonathan Swift)

lest CONJ in case. If you do something lest something (usually) unpleasant happens you do it to try to prevent it happening ❑ *She went in without knocking, and hurried upstairs, in great fear lest she should meet the real Mary Ann* (Alice's Adventures in Wonderland by Lewis Carroll)

levee NOUN a levee is an old term for a meeting held in the morning, shortly after the person holding the meeting has got out of bed ❑ *I used to attend the King's levee once or twice a week* (Gulliver's Travels by Jonathan Swift)

life-preserver NOUN a club which had lead inside it to make it heavier and therefore more dangerous ❑ *and with no more suspicious articles displayed to view than two or three heavy bludgeons which stood in a corner, and a "life-preserver" that hung over the chimney-piece.* (Oliver Twist by Charles Dickens)

lighterman NOUN a lighterman is another word for sailor ❑ *in and out, hammers going in ship-builders' yards, saws going at timber, clashing engines going at things unknown, pumps going in leaky ships, capstans going, ships going out to sea, and unintelligible sea creatures roaring curses over the bulwarks at respondent lightermen* (Great Expectations by Charles Dickens)

livery NOUN servants often wore a uniform known as a livery ❑ *suddenly a footman in livery came running out of the wood* (Alice's Adventures in Wonderland by Lewis Carroll)

livid ADJ livid means pale or ash coloured. Livid also means very angry ❑ *a dirty, livid white* (Treasure Island by Robert Louis Stevenson)

lottery-tickets NOUN a popular card game ❑ *and Mrs Philips protested that they would have a nice comfortable noisy game of lottery tickets* (Pride and Prejudice by Jane Austen)

lower and upper world PHRASE the earth and the heavens are the lower and upper worlds ❑ *the changes in the lower and upper world* (Gulliver's Travels by Jonathan Swift)

lustres NOUN lustres are chandeliers. A chandelier is a large, decorative frame which holds light bulbs or candles and hangs from the ceiling ❑ *the lustres, lights, the carving and the guilding* (The Prelude by William Wordsworth)

lynched VERB killed without a criminal trial by a crowd of people ❑ *He'll never know how nigh he come to getting lynched* (The Adventures of Huckleberry Finn by Mark Twain)

malingering VERB if someone is malingering they are pretending to be ill to avoid working ❑ *And you stand there malingering* (Treasure Island by Robert Louis Stevenson)

managing PHRASE treating with consideration ❑ *to think the honour of my own kind not worth managing* (Gulliver's Travels by Jonathan Swift)

manhood PHRASE manhood means human nature ❑ *concerning the nature of manhood* (Gulliver's Travels by Jonathan Swift)

man-trap NOUN a man-trap is a set of steel jaws that snap shut when trodden on and trap a person's leg

❏ *"Don't go to him," I called out of the window, "he's an assassin! A man-trap!"* (Oliver Twist by Charles Dickens)

maps NOUN charts of the night sky ❏ *Let maps to others, worlds on worlds have shown* (The Good-Morrow by John Donne)

mark VERB look at or notice ❏ *Mark but this flea, and mark in this* (The Flea by John Donne)

maroons NOUN A maroon is someone who has been left in a place which it is difficult for them to escape from, like a small island ❏ *if schooners, islands, and maroons* (Treasure Island by Robert Louis Stevenson)

mast NOUN here mast means the fruit of forest trees ❏ *a quantity of acorns, dates, chestnuts, and other mast* (Gulliver's Travels by Jonathan Swift)

mate VERB defeat ❏ *Where Mars did mate the warlike Carthigens* (Doctor Faustus Chorus by Christopher Marlowe)

mealy ADJ Mealy when used to describe a face meant pallid, pale or colourless ❏ *I only know two sorts of boys. Mealy boys, and beef-faced boys* (Oliver Twist by Charles Dickens)

middling ADV fairly or moderately ❏ *she worked me middling hard for about an hour* (The Adventures of Huckleberry Finn by Mark Twain)

mill NOUN a mill, or treadmill, was a device for hard labour or punishment in prison ❏ *Was you never on the mill?* (Oliver Twist by Charles Dickens)

milliner's shop NOUN a milliner's sold fabrics, clothing, lace and accessories; as time went on they specialized more and more in hats ❏ *to pay their duty to their aunt and to a milliner's shop just over the way* (Pride and Prejudice by Jane Austen)

minching un' munching PHRASE how people in the north of England used to describe the way people from the south speak ❏ *Minching un' munching!* (Wuthering Heights by Emily Brontë)

mine NOUN gold ❏ *Whether both th'Indias of spice and mine* (The Sun Rising by John Donne)

mire NOUN mud ❏ *Tis my fate to be always ground into the mire under the iron heel of oppression* (The Adventures of Huckleberry Finn by Mark Twain)

miscellany NOUN a miscellany is a collection of many different kinds of things ❏ *under that, the miscellany began* (Treasure Island by Robert Louis Stevenson)

mistarshers NOUN mistarshers means moustache, which is the hair that grows on a man's upper lip ❏ *when he put his hand up to his mistarshers* (Tess of the D'Urbervilles by Thomas Hardy)

morrow NOUN here good-morrow means tomorrow and a new and better life ❏ *And now good-morrow to our waking souls* (The Good-Morrow by John Donne)

mortification NOUN mortification is an old word for gangrene which is when part of the body decays or "dies" because of disease ❏ *Yes, it was a mortification–that was it* (The Adventures of Huckleberry Finn by Mark Twain)

mought VERB mought is an old spelling of might ❏ *what you mought call me? You mought call me captain* (Treasure Island by Robert Louis Stevenson)

move VERB move me not means do not make me angry ❏ *Move me not, Faustus* (Doctor Faustus 2.1 by Christopher Marlowe)

muffin-cap NOUN a muffin-cap is a flat cap made from wool ❏ *the old one, remained stationary in the muffin-cap and leathers* (Oliver Twist by Charles Dickens)

mulatter NOUN a mulatter was another word for mulatto, which is a person with parents who are from different races ❑ *a mulatter, most as white as a white man* (The Adventures of Huckleberry Finn by Mark Twain)

mummery NOUN mummery is an old word that meant meaningless (or pretentious) ceremony ❑ *When they were all gone, and when Trabb and his men–but not his boy: I looked for him–had crammed their mummery into bags, and were gone too, the house felt wholesomer.* (Great Expectations by Charles Dickens)

nap NOUN the nap is the woolly surface on a new item of clothing. Here the surface has been worn away so it looks bare ❑ *like an old hat with the nap rubbed off* (The Adventures of Huckleberry Finn by Mark Twain)

natural ■ NOUN a natural is a person born with learning difficulties ❑ *though he had been left to his particular care by their deceased father, who thought him almost a natural.* (David Copperfield by Charles Dickens) ■ ADJ natural meant illegitimate ❑ *Harriet Smith was the natural daughter of somebody* (Emma by Jane Austen)

navigator NOUN a navigator was originally someone employed to dig canals. It is the origin of the word "navvy" meaning a labourer ❑ *She ascertained from me in a few words what it was all about, comforted Dora, and gradually convinced her that I was not a labourer–from my manner of stating the case I believe Dora concluded that I was a navigator, and went balancing myself up and down a plank all day with a wheelbarrow–and so brought us together in peace.* (David Copperfield by Charles Dickens)

necromancy NOUN necromancy means a kind of magic where the magician speaks to spirits or ghosts to find out what will happen in the future ❑ *He surfeits upon cursed necromancy* (Doctor Faustus chorus by Christopher Marlowe)

negus NOUN a negus is a hot drink made from sweetened wine and water ❑ *He sat placidly perusing the newspaper, with his little head on one side, and a glass of warm sherry negus at his elbow.* (David Copperfield by Charles Dickens)

nice ADJ discriminating. Able to make good judgements or choices ❑ *consequently a claim to be nice* (Emma by Jane Austen)

nigh ADV nigh means near ❑ *He'll never know how nigh he come to getting lynched* (The Adventures of Huckleberry Finn by Mark Twain)

nimbleness NOUN nimbleness means being able to move very quickly or skilfully ❑ *and with incredible accuracy and nimbleness* (Treasure Island by Robert Louis Stevenson)

noggin NOUN a noggin is a small mug or a wooden cup ❑ *you'll bring me one noggin of rum* (Treasure Island by Robert Louis Stevenson)

none ADJ neither ❑ *none can die* (The Good-Morrow by John Donne)

notices NOUN observations ❑ *Arch are his notices* (The Prelude by William Wordsworth)

occiput NOUN occiput means the back of the head ❑ *saw off the occiput of each couple* (Gulliver's Travels by Jonathan Swift)

officiously ADV kindly ❑ *the governess who attended Glumdalclitch very officiously lifted me up* (Gulliver's Travels by Jonathan Swift)

old salt PHRASE old salt is a slang term for an experienced sailor ❑ *a "true sea-dog", and a "real old salt"* (Treasure Island by Robert Louis Stevenson)

or ere PHRASE before ❑ *or ere the Hall was built* (The Prelude by William Wordsworth)

ostler NOUN one who looks after horses at an inn ❑ *The bill paid, and the waiter remembered, and the ostler not forgotten, and the chambermaid taken into consideration* (Great Expectations by Charles Dickens)

ostry NOUN an ostry is an old word for a pub or hotel ❑ *lest I send you into the ostry with a vengeance* (Doctor Faustus 2.2 by Christopher Marlowe)

outrunning the constable PHRASE outrunning the constable meant spending more than you earn ❑ *but I shall by this means be able to check your bills and to pull you up if I find you outrunning the constable.* (Great Expectations by Charles Dickens)

over ADV across ❑ *It is in length six yards, and in the thickest part at least three yards over* (Gulliver's Travels by Jonathan Swift)

over the broomstick PHRASE this is a phrase meaning "getting married without a formal ceremony" ❑ *They both led tramping lives, and this woman in Gerrard-street here, had been married very young, over the broomstick (as we say), to a tramping man, and was a perfect fury in point of jealousy.* (Great Expectations by Charles Dickens)

own VERB own means to admit or to acknowledge ❑ *It's my old girl that advises. She has the head. But I never own to it before her. Discipline must be maintained* (Bleak House by Charles Dickens)

page NOUN here page means a boy employed to run errands ❑ *not my feigned page* (On His Mistress by John Donne)

paid pretty dear PHRASE paid pretty dear means paid a high price or suffered quite a lot ❑ *I paid pretty dear for my monthly fourpenny piece* (Treasure Island by Robert Louis Stevenson)

pannikins NOUN pannikins were small tin cups ❑ *of lifting light glasses and cups to his lips, as if they were clumsy pannikins* (Great Expectations by Charles Dickens)

pards NOUN pards are leopards ❑ *Not charioted by Bacchus and his pards* (Ode to a Nightingale by John Keats)

parlour boarder NOUN a pupil who lived with the family ❑ *and somebody had lately raised her from the condition of scholar to parlour boarder* (Emma by Jane Austen)

particular, a London PHRASE London in Victorian times and up to the 1950s was famous for having very dense fog–which was a combination of real fog and the smog of pollution from factories ❑ *This is a London particular . . . A fog, miss* (Bleak House by Charles Dickens)

patten NOUN pattens were wooden soles which were fixed to shoes by straps to protect the shoes in wet weather ❑ *carrying a basket like the Great Seal of England in plaited straw, a pair of pattens, a spare shawl, and an umbrella, though it was a fine bright day* (Great Expectations by Charles Dickens)

paviour NOUN a paviour was a labourer who worked on the street pavement ❑ *the paviour his pickaxe* (Oliver Twist by Charles Dickens)

peccant ADJ peccant means unhealthy ❑ *other peccant humours* (Gulliver's Travels by Jonathan Swift)

penetralium NOUN penetralium is a word used to describe the inner rooms of the house ❑ *and I had no desire to aggravate his impatience previous to inspecting the penetralium* (Wuthering Heights by Emily Brontë)

pensive ADV pensive means deep in thought or thinking seriously about something ❑ *and she was leaning pensive on a tomb-stone on her right elbow* (The Adventures of Huckleberry Finn by Mark Twain)

penury NOUN penury is the state of being extremely poor ❑ *Distress, if not penury, loomed in the distance* (Tess of the D'Urbervilles by Thomas Hardy)

perspective NOUN telescope ❑ *a pocket perspective* (Gulliver's Travels by Jonathan Swift)

phaeton NOUN a phaeton was an open carriage for four people ❑ *often* *condescends to drive by my humble abode in her little phaeton and ponies* (Pride and Prejudice by Jane Austen)

phantasm NOUN a phantasm is an illusion, something that is not real. It is sometimes used to mean ghost ❑ *Experience had bred no fancies in him that could raise the phantasm of appetite* (Silas Marner by George Eliot)

physic NOUN here physic means medicine ❑ *there I studied physic two years and seven months* (Gulliver's Travels by Jonathan Swift)

pinioned VERB to pinion is to hold both arms so that a person cannot move them ❑ *But the relentless Ghost pinioned him in both his arms, and forced him to observe what happened next.* (A Christmas Carol by Charles Dickens)

piquet NOUN piquet was a popular card game in the C18th ❑ *Mr Hurst and Mr Bingley were at piquet* (Pride and Prejudice by Jane Austen)

plaister NOUN a plaister is a piece of cloth on which an apothecary (or pharmacist) would spread ointment. The cloth is then applied to wounds or bruises to treat them ❑ *Then, she gave the knife a final smart wipe on the edge of the plaister, and then sawed a very thick round off the loaf: which she finally, before separating from the loaf, hewed into two halves, of which Joe got one, and I the other.* (Great Expectations by Charles Dickens)

plantations NOUN here plantations means colonies, which are countries controlled by a more powerful country ❑ *besides our plantations in America* (Gulliver's Travels by Jonathan Swift)

plastic ADJ here plastic is an old term meaning shaping or a power that was forming ❑ *A plastic power abode with me* (The Prelude by William Wordsworth)

players NOUN actors ❑ *of players which upon the world's stage be* (On His Mistress by John Donne)

SIR GAWAIN AND THE GREEN KNIGHT

plump ADV all at once, suddenly ❑ *But it took a bit of time to get it well round, the change come so uncommon plump, didn't it?* (Great Expectations by Charles Dickens)

plundered VERB to plunder is to rob or steal from ❑ *These crosses stand for the names of ships or towns that they sank or plundered* (Treasure Island by Robert Louis Stevenson)

pommel ■ VERB to pommel someone is to hit them repeatedly with your fists ❑ *hug him round the neck, pommel his back, and kick his legs in irrepressible affection!* (A Christmas Carol by Charles Dickens) ■ NOUN a pommel is the part of a saddle that rises up at the front ❑ *He had his gun across his pommel* (The Adventures of Huckleberry Finn by Mark Twain)

poor's rates NOUN poor's rates were property taxes which were used to support the poor ❑ *"Oh!" replied the undertaker; "why, you know, Mr. Bumble, I pay a good deal towards the poor's rates."* (Oliver Twist by Charles Dickens)

popular ADJ popular means ruled by the people, or Republican, rather than ruled by a monarch ❑ *With those of Greece compared and popular Rome* (The Prelude by William Wordsworth)

porringer NOUN a porringer is a small bowl ❑ *Of this festive composition each boy had one porringer, and no more* (Oliver Twist by Charles Dickens)

postboy NOUN a postboy was the driver of a horse-drawn carriage ❑ *He spoke to a postboy who was dozing under the gateway* (Oliver Twist by Charles Dickens)

post-chaise NOUN a fast carriage for two or four passengers ❑ *Looking round, he saw that it was a post-chaise, driven at great speed* (Oliver Twist by Charles Dickens)

postern NOUN a small gate usually at the back of a building ❑ *The little servant happening to be entering the* *fortress with two hot rolls, I passed through the postern and crossed the drawbridge, in her company* (Great Expectations by Charles Dickens)

pottle NOUN a pottle was a small basket ❑ *He had a paper-bag under each arm and a pottle of strawberries in one hand . . .* (Great Expectations by Charles Dickens)

pounce NOUN pounce is a fine powder used to prevent ink spreading on untreated paper ❑ *in that grim atmosphere of pounce and parchment, red-tape, dusty wafers, ink-jars, brief and draft paper, law reports, writs, declarations, and bills of costs* (David Copperfield by Charles Dickens)

pox NOUN pox means sexually transmitted diseases like syphilis ❑ *how the pox in all its consequences and denominations* (Gulliver's Travels by Jonathan Swift)

prelibation NOUN prelibation means a foretaste of or an example of something to come ❑ *A prelibation to the mower's scythe* (The Prelude by William Wordsworth)

prentice NOUN an apprentice ❑ *and Joe, sitting on an old gun, had told me that when I was 'prentice to him regularly bound, we would have such Larks there!* (Great Expectations by Charles Dickens)

presently ADV immediately ❑ *I presently knew what they meant* (Gulliver's Travels by Jonathan Swift)

pumpion NOUN pumpkin ❑ *for it was almost as large as a small pumpion* (Gulliver's Travels by Jonathan Swift)

punctual ADJ kept in one place ❑ *was not a punctual presence, but a spirit* (The Prelude by William Wordsworth)

quadrille NOUN a quadrille is a dance invented in France which is usually performed by four couples ❑ *However, Mr Swiveller had Miss Sophy's hand for the first quadrille (country-dances being low, were utterly proscribed)* (The Old Curiosity Shop by Charles Dickens) ■ NOUN quadrille was a card game for four people ❑ *to make up her pool of quadrille in the evening* (Pride and Prejudice by Jane Austen)

quality NOUN gentry or upper-class people ❑ *if you are with the quality* (The Adventures of Huckleberry Finn by Mark Twain)

quick parts PHRASE quick-witted ❑ *Mr Bennet was so odd a mixture of quick parts* (Pride and Prejudice by Jane Austen)

quid NOUN a quid is something chewed or kept in the mouth, like a piece of tobacco ❑ *rolling his quid* (Treasure Island by Robert Louis Stevenson)

quit VERB quit means to avenge or to make even ❑ *But Faustus's death shall quit my infamy* (Doctor Faustus 4.3 by Christopher Marlowe)

rags NOUN divisions ❑ *Nor hours, days, months, which are the rags of time* (The Sun Rising by John Donne)

raiment NOUN raiment means clothing ❑ *the mountain shook off turf and flower, had only heath for raiment and crag for gem* (Jane Eyre by Charlotte Brontë)

rain cats and dogs PHRASE an expression meaning rain heavily. The origin of the expression is unclear ❑ *But it'll perhaps rain cats and dogs to-morrow* (Silas Marner by George Eliot)

raised Cain PHRASE raised Cain means caused a lot of trouble. Cain is a character in the Bible who killed his brother Abel ❑ *and every time he got drunk he raised Cain around town* (The Adventures of Huckleberry Finn by Mark Twain)

rambling ADJ rambling means confused and not very clear ❑ *my head began to be filled very early with rambling thoughts* (Robinson Crusoe by Daniel Defoe)

raree-show NOUN a raree-show is an old term for a peep-show or a fairground entertainment ❑ *A raree-show is here, with children gathered round* (The Prelude by William Wordsworth)

recusants NOUN people who resisted authority ❑ *hardy recusants* (The Prelude by William Wordsworth)

redounding VERB eddying. An eddy is a movement in water or air which goes round and round instead of flowing in one direction ❑ *mists and steam-like fogs redounding everywhere* (The Prelude by William Wordsworth)

redundant ADJ here redundant means overflowing but Wordsworth also uses it to mean excessively large or too big ❑ *A tempest, a redundant energy* (The Prelude by William Wordsworth)

reflex NOUN reflex is a shortened version of reflexion, which is an alternative spelling of reflection ❑ *To cut across the reflex of a star* (The Prelude by William Wordsworth)

Reformatory NOUN a prison for young offenders/criminals ❑ *Even when I was taken to have a new suit of clothes, the tailor had orders to make them like a kind of Reformatory, and on no account to let me have the free use of my limbs.* (Great Expectations by Charles Dickens)

remorse NOUN pity or compassion ❑ *by that remorse* (On His Mistress by John Donne)

render VERB in this context render means give. ❑ *and Sarah could render no reason that would be sanctioned by the feeling of the community.* (Silas Marner by George Eliot)

repeater NOUN a repeater was a watch that chimed the last hour when a button was pressed–as a result it was useful in the dark ❑ *And his watch is a gold repeater, and worth a hundred pound if it's worth a penny.* (Great Expectations by Charles Dickens)

repugnance NOUN repugnance means a strong dislike of something or someone ❑ *overcoming a strong repugnance* (Treasure Island by Robert Louis Stevenson)

reverence NOUN reverence means bow. When you bow to someone, you briefly bend your body towards them as a formal way of showing them respect ❑ *made my reverence* (Gulliver's Travels by Jonathan Swift)

reverie NOUN a reverie is a daydream ❑ *I can guess the subject of your reverie* (Pride and Prejudice by Jane Austen)

revival NOUN a religious meeting held in public ❑ *well I'd ben a-running' a little temperance revival thar' bout a week* (The Adventures of Huckleberry Finn by Mark Twain)

revolt VERB revolt means turn back or stop your present course of action and go back to what you were doing before ❑ *Revolt, or I'll in piecemeal tear thy flesh* (Doctor Faustus 5.1 by Christopher Marlowe)

rheumatics/rheumatism NOUN rheumatics [rheumatism] is an illness that makes your joints or muscles stiff and painful ❑ *a new cure for the rheumatics* (Treasure Island by Robert Louis Stevenson)

riddance NOUN riddance is usually used in the form good riddance which you say when you are pleased that something has gone or been left behind ❑ *I'd better go into the house, and die and be a riddance* (David Copperfield by Charles Dickens)

rimy ADJ rimy is an adjective which means covered in ice or frost ❑ *It was a rimy morning, and very damp* (Great Expectations by Charles Dickens)

riper ADJ riper means more mature or older ❑ *At riper years to Wittenberg he went* (Doctor Faustus chorus by Christopher Marlowe)

TRANSLATED BY JESSIE WESTON

rubber NOUN a set of games in whist or backgammon ❑ *her father was sure of his rubber* (*Emma* by Jane Austen)

ruffian NOUN a ruffian is a person who behaves violently ❑ *and when the ruffian had told him* (*Treasure Island* by Robert Louis Stevenson)

sadness NOUN sadness is an old term meaning seriousness ❑ *But I prithee tell me, in good sadness* (*Doctor Faustus 2.2* by Christopher Marlowe)

sailed before the mast PHRASE this phrase meant someone who did not look like a sailor ❑ *he had none of the appearance of a man that sailed before the mast* (*Treasure Island* by Robert Louis Stevenson)

scabbard NOUN a scabbard is the covering for a sword or dagger ❑ *Girded round its middle was an antique scabbard; but no sword was in it, and the ancient sheath was eaten up with rust* (*A Christmas Carol* by Charles Dickens)

schooners NOUN A schooner is a fast, medium-sized sailing ship ❑ *if schooners, islands, and maroons* (*Treasure Island* by Robert Louis Stevenson)

science NOUN learning or knowledge ❑ *Even Science, too, at hand* (*The Prelude* by William Wordsworth)

scrouge VERB to scrouge means to squeeze or to crowd ❑ *to scrouge in and get a sight* (*The Adventures of Huckleberry Finn* by Mark Twain)

scrutore NOUN a scrutore, or escritoire, was a writing table ❑ *set me gently on my feet upon the scrutore* (*Gulliver's Travels* by Jonathan Swift)

scutcheon/escutcheon NOUN an escutcheon is a shield with a coat of arms, or the symbols of a family name, engraved on it ❑ *On the scutcheon we'll have a bend* (*The Adventures of Huckleberry Finn* by Mark Twain)

sea-dog PHRASE sea-dog is a slang term for an experienced sailor or pirate ❑ *a "true sea-dog", and a "real old salt,"* (*Treasure Island* by Robert Louis Stevenson)

see the lions PHRASE to see the lions was to go and see the sights of London. Originally the phrase referred to the menagerie in the Tower of London and later in Regent's Park ❑ *We will go and see the lions for an hour or two—it's something to have a fresh fellow like you to show them to, Copperfield* (*David Copperfield* by Charles Dickens)

self-conceit NOUN self-conceit is an old term which means having to high an opinion of oneself, or deceiving yourself ❑ *Till swollen with cunning, of a self-conceit* (*Doctor Faustus chorus* by Christopher Marlowe)

seneschal NOUN a steward ❑ *where a grey-headed seneschal sings a funny chorus with a funnier body of vassals* (*Oliver Twist* by Charles Dickens)

sensible ADJ if you were sensible of something you are aware or conscious of something ❑ *If my children are silly I must hope to be always sensible of it* (*Pride and Prejudice* by Jane Austen)

sessions NOUN court cases were heard at specific times of the year called sessions ❑ *He lay in prison very ill, during the whole interval between his committal for trial, and the coming round of the Sessions.* (*Great Expectations* by Charles Dickens)

shabby ADJ shabby places look old and in bad condition ❑ *a little bit of a shabby village named Pikesville* (*The Adventures of Huckleberry Finn* by Mark Twain)

shay-cart NOUN a shay-cart was a small cart drawn by one horse ❑ *"I were at the Bargemen t'other night, Pip;" whenever he subsided into affection, he called me Pip, and whenever he relapsed into politeness he called me Sir; "when there come up in his* shay-cart Pumblechook." (*Great Expectations* by Charles Dickens)

shilling NOUN a shilling is an old unit of currency. There were twenty shillings in every British pound ❑ *"Ten shillings too much," said the gentleman in the white waistcoat.* (*Oliver Twist* by Charles Dickens)

shines NOUN tricks or games ❑ *well, it would make a cow laugh to see the shines that old idiot cut* (*The Adventures of Huckleberry Finn* by Mark Twain)

shirking VERB shirking means not doing what you are meant to be doing, or evading your duties ❑ *some of you shirking lubbers* (*Treasure Island* by Robert Louis Stevenson)

shiver my timbers PHRASE shiver my timbers is an expression which was used by sailors and pirates to express surprise ❑ *why, shiver my timbers, if I hadn't forgotten my score!* (*Treasure Island* by Robert Louis Stevenson)

shoe-roses NOUN shoe-roses were roses made from ribbons which were stuck on to shoes as decoration ❑ *the very shoe-roses for Netherfield were got by proxy* (*Pride and Prejudice* by Jane Austen)

singular ADJ singular means very great and remarkable or strange ❑ *"Singular dream," he says* (*The Adventures of Huckleberry Finn* by Mark Twain)

sire NOUN sire is an old word which means lord or master or elder ❑ *She also defied her sire* (*Little Women* by Louisa May Alcott)

sixpence NOUN a sixpence was half of a shilling ❑ *if she had only a shilling in the world, she would be very lilkely to give away sixpence of it* (*Emma* by Jane Austen)

slavey NOUN the word slavey was used when there was only one servant in a house or boarding-house—so she had to perform all the duties of a larger staff ❑ *Two distinct knocks, sir, will produce the slavey at any time* (*The Old Curiosity Shop* by Charles Dickens)

slender ADJ weak ❑ *In slender accents of sweet verse* (*The Prelude* by William Wordsworth)

slop-shops NOUN slop-shops were shops where cheap ready-made clothes were sold. They mainly sold clothes to sailors ❑ *Accordingly, I took the jacket off, that I might learn to do without it; and carrying it under my arm, began a tour of inspection of the various slop-shops.* (*David Copperfield* by Charles Dickens)

sluggard NOUN a lazy person ❑ *"Stand up and repeat 'Tis the voice of the sluggard,'" said the Gryphon.* (*Alice's Adventures in Wonderland* by Lewis Carroll)

smallpox NOUN smallpox is a serious infectious disease ❑ *by telling the men we had smallpox aboard* (*The Adventures of Huckleberry Finn* by Mark Twain)

smalls NOUN smalls are short trousers ❑ *It is difficult for a large-headed, small-eyed youth, of lumbering make and heavy countenance, to look dignified under any circumstances; but it is more especially so, when superadded to these personal attractions are a red nose and yellow smalls* (*Oliver Twist* by Charles Dickens)

sneeze-box NOUN a box for snuff was called a sneeze-box because sniffing snuff makes the user sneeze ❑ *To think of Jack Dawkins—lummy Jack—the Dodger—the Artful Dodger—going abroad for a common twopenny-halfpenny sneeze-box!* (*Oliver Twist* by Charles Dickens)

snorted VERB slept ❑ *Or snorted we in the Seven Sleepers' den?* (*The Good-Morrow* by John Donne)

snuff NOUN snuff is tobacco in powder form which is taken by sniffing ❑ *as he thrust his thumb and forefinger into the proffered snuff-box of the undertaker: which was an ingenious little model of a patent* coffin. (*Oliver Twist* by Charles Dickens)

soliloquized VERB to soliloquize is when an actor in a play speaks to himself or herself rather than to another actor ❏ *"A new servitude! There is something in that," I soliloquized (mentally, be it understood; I did not talk aloud)* (*Jane Eyre* by Charlotte Brontë)

sough NOUN a sough is a drain or a ditch ❏ *as you may have noticed the sough that runs from the marshes* (*Wuthering Heights* by Emily Brontë)

spirits NOUN a spirit is the nonphysical part of a person which is believed to remain alive after their death ❏ *that I might raise up spirits when I please* (*Doctor Faustus 1.5* by Christopher Marlowe)

spleen ■ NOUN here spleen means a type of sadness or depression which was thought to only affect the wealthy ❏ *yet here I could plainly discover the true seeds of spleen* (*Gulliver's Travels* by Jonathan Swift) ■ NOUN irritability and low spirits ❏ *Adieu to disappointment and spleen* (*Pride and Prejudice* by Jane Austen)

spondulicks NOUN spondulicks is a slang word which means money ❏ *not for all his spondulicks and as much more on top of it* (*The Adventures of Huckleberry Finn* by Mark Twain)

stalled of VERB to be stalled of something is to be bored with it ❏ *I'm stalled of doing naught* (*Wuthering Heights* by Emily Brontë)

stanchion NOUN a stanchion is a pole or bar that stands upright and is used as a building support ❏ *and slid down a stanchion* (*The Adventures of Huckleberry Finn* by Mark Twain)

stang NOUN stang is another word for pole which was an old measurement ❏ *These fields were intermingled with woods of half a stang* (*Gulliver's Travels* by Jonathan Swift)

starlings NOUN a starling is a wall built around the pillars that support a bridge to protect the pillars ❏ *There were states of the tide when, having been down the river, I could not get back through the eddy-chafed arches and starlings of old London Bridge* (*Great Expectations* by Charles Dickens)

startings NOUN twitching or night-time movements of the body ❏ *with midnight's startings* (*On His Mistress* by John Donne)

stomacher NOUN a panel at the front of a dress ❏ *but send her aunt the pattern of a stomacher* (*Emma* by Jane Austen)

stoop VERB swoop ❏ *Once a kite hovering over the garden made a stoop at me* (*Gulliver's Travels* by Jonathan Swift)

succedaneum NOUN a succedaneum is a substitute ❏ *But as a succedaneum* (*The Prelude* by William Wordsworth)

suet NOUN a hard animal fat used in cooking ❏ *and your jaws are too weak For anything tougher than suet* (*Alice's Adventures in Wonderland* by Lewis Carroll)

sultry ADJ sultry weather is hot and damp. Here sultry means unpleasant or risky ❏ *for it was getting pretty sultry for us* (*The Adventures of Huckleberry Finn* by Mark Twain)

summerset NOUN summerset is an old spelling of somersault. If someone does a somersault, they turn over completely in the air ❏ *I have seen him do the summerset* (*Gulliver's Travels* by Jonathan Swift)

supper NOUN supper was a light meal taken late in the evening. The main meal was dinner which was eaten at four or five in the afternoon ❏ *and the supper table was all set out* (*Emma* by Jane Austen)

surfeits VERB to surfeit in something is to have far too much of it, or to overindulge in it to an unhealthy degree ❏ *He surfeits upon cursed*

necromancy (*Doctor Faustus* chorus by Christopher Marlowe)

surtout NOUN a surtout is a long close-fitting overcoat ❑ *He wore a long black surtout reaching nearly to his ankles* (*The Old Curiosity Shop* by Charles Dickens)

swath NOUN swath is the width of corn cut by a scythe ❑ *while thy hook Spares the next swath* (*Ode to Autumn* by John Keats)

sylvan ADJ sylvan means belonging to the woods ❑ *Sylvan historian* (*Ode on a Grecian Urn* by John Keats)

taction NOUN taction means touch. This means that the people had to be touched on the mouth or the ears to get their attention ❑ *without being roused by some external taction upon the organs of speech and hearing* (*Gulliver's Travels* by Jonathan Swift)

Tag and Rag and Bobtail PHRASE the riff-raff, or lower classes. Used in an insulting way ❑ *"No," said he; "not till it got about that there was no protection on the premises, and it come to be considered dangerous, with convicts and Tag and Rag and Bobtail going up and down."* (*Great Expectations* by Charles Dickens)

tallow NOUN tallow is hard animal fat that is used to make candles and soap ❑ *and a lot of tallow candles* (*The Adventures of Huckleberry Finn* by Mark Twain)

tan VERB to tan means to beat or whip ❑ *and if I catch you about that school I'll tan you good* (*The Adventures of Huckleberry Finn* by Mark Twain)

tanyard NOUN the tanyard is part of a tannery, which is a place where leather is made from animal skins ❑ *hid in the old tanyard* (*The Adventures of Huckleberry Finn* by Mark Twain)

tarry ADJ tarry means the colour of tar or black ❑ *his tarry pig-tail* (*Treasure Island* by Robert Louis Stevenson)

thereof PHRASE from there ❑ *By all desires which thereof did ensue* (*On His Mistress* by John Donne)

thick with, be PHRASE if you are "thick with someone" you are very close, sharing secrets–it is often used to describe people who are planning something secret ❑ *Hasn't he been thick with Mr Heathcliff lately?* (*Wuthering Heights* by Emily Brontë)

thimble NOUN a thimble is a small cover used to protect the finger while sewing ❑ *The paper had been sealed in several places by a thimble* (*Treasure Island* by Robert Louis Stevenson)

thirtover ADJ thirtover is an old word which means obstinate or that someone is very determined to do want they want and can not be persuaded to do something in another way ❑ *I have been living on in a thirtover, lackadaisical way* (*Tess of the D'Urbervilles* by Thomas Hardy)

timbrel NOUN timbrel is a tambourine ❑ *What pipes and timbrels?* (*Ode on a Grecian Urn* by John Keats)

tin NOUN tin is slang for money/cash ❑ *Then the plain question is, an't it a pity that this state of things should continue, and how much better would it be for the old gentleman to hand over a reasonable amount of tin, and make it all right and comfortable* (*The Old Curiosity Shop* by Charles Dickens)

tincture NOUN a tincture is a medicine made with alcohol and a small amount of a drug ❑ *with ink composed of a cephalic tincture* (*Gulliver's Travels* by Jonathan Swift)

tithe NOUN a tithe is a tax paid to the church ❑ *and held farms which, speaking from a spiritual point of view, paid highly-desirable tithes* (*Silas Marner* by George Eliot)

TRANSLATED BY JESSIE WESTON

towardly ADJ a towardly child is dutiful or obedient ❑ *and a towardly child* (*Gulliver's Travels* by Jonathan Swift)

toys NOUN trifles are things which are considered to have little importance, value, or significance ❑ *purchase my life from them by some bracelets, glass rings, and other toys* (*Gulliver's Travels* by Jonathan Swift)

tract NOUN a tract is a religious pamphlet or leaflet ❑ *and Joe Harper got a hymn-book and a tract* (*The Adventures of Huckleberry Finn* by Mark Twain)

train-oil NOUN train-oil is oil from whale blubber ❑ *The train-oil and gunpowder were shoved out of sight in a minute* (*Wuthering Heights* by Emily Brontë)

tribulation NOUN tribulation means the suffering or difficulty you experience in a particular situation ❑ *Amy was learning this distinction through much tribulation* (*Little Women* by Louisa May Alcott)

trivet NOUN a trivet is a three-legged stand for resting a pot or kettle ❑ *a pocket-knife in his right; and a pewter pot on the trivet* (*Oliver Twist* by Charles Dickens)

trot line NOUN a trot line is a fishing line to which a row of smaller fishing lines are attached ❑ *when he got along I was hard at it taking up a trot line* (*The Adventures of Huckleberry Finn* by Mark Twain)

troth NOUN oath or pledge ❑ *I wonder, by my troth* (*The Good-Morrow* by John Donne)

truckle NOUN a truckle bedstead is a bed that is on wheels and can be slid under another bed to save space ❑ *It rose under my hand, and the door yielded. Looking in, I saw a lighted candle on a table, a bench, and a mattress on a truckle bedstead.* (*Great Expectations* by Charles Dickens)

trump NOUN a trump is a good, reliable person who can be trusted ❑ *This lad Hawkins is a trump, I perceive* (*Treasure Island* by Robert Louis Stevenson)

tucker NOUN a tucker is a frilly lace collar which is worn around the neck ❑ *Whereat Scrooge's niece's sister—the plump one with the lace tucker: not the one with the roses—blushed.* (*A Christmas Carol* by Charles Dickens)

tureen NOUN a large bowl with a lid from which soup or vegetables are served ❑ *Waiting in a hot tureen!* (*Alice's Adventures in Wonderland* by Lewis Carroll)

turnkey NOUN a prison officer; jailer ❑ *As we came out of the prison through the lodge, I found that the great importance of my guardian was appreciated by the turnkeys, no less than by those whom they held in charge.* (*Great Expectations* by Charles Dickens)

turnpike NOUN the upkeep of many roads of the time was paid for by tolls (fees) collected at posts along the road. There was a gate to prevent people travelling further along the road until the toll had been paid. ❑ *Traddles, whom I have taken up by appointment at the turnpike, presents a dazzling combination of cream colour and light blue; and both he and Mr. Dick have a general effect about them of being all gloves.* (*David Copperfield* by Charles Dickens)

twas PHRASE it was ❑ *twas but a dream of thee* (*The Good-Morrow* by John Donne)

tyrannized VERB tyrannized means bullied or forced to do things against their will ❑ *for people would soon cease coming there to be tyrannized over and put down* (*Treasure Island* by Robert Louis Stevenson)

'un NOUN 'un is a slang term for one—usually used to refer to a person ❑ *She's been thinking the old 'un* (*David Copperfield* by Charles Dickens)

undistinguished ADJ undiscriminating or incapable of making a distinction between good and bad things ❑

their undistinguished appetite to devour everything (*Gulliver's Travels* by Jonathan Swift)

use NOUN habit ❑ *Though use make you apt to kill me* (*The Flea* by John Donne)

vacant ADJ vacant usually means empty, but here Wordsworth uses it to mean carefree ❑ *To vacant musing, unreproved neglect* (*The Prelude* by William Wordsworth)

valetudinarian NOUN one too concerned with his or her own health. ❑ *for having been a valetudinarian all his life* (*Emma* by Jane Austen)

vamp VERB vamp means to walk or tramp to somewhere ❑ *Well, vamp on to Marlott, will 'ee* (*Tess of the D'Urbervilles* by Thomas Hardy)

vapours NOUN the vapours is an old term which means unpleasant and strange thoughts, which make the person feel nervous and unhappy ❑ *and my head was full of vapours* (*Robinson Crusoe* by Daniel Defoe)

vegetables NOUN here vegetables means plants ❑ *the other vegetables are in the same proportion* (*Gulliver's Travels* by Jonathan Swift)

venturesome ADJ if you are venturesome you are willing to take risks ❑ *he must be either hopelessly stupid or a venturesome fool* (*Wuthering Heights* by Emily Brontë)

verily ADV verily means really or truly ❑ *though I believe verily* (*Robinson Crusoe* by Daniel Defoe)

vicinage NOUN vicinage is an area or the residents of an area ❑ *and to his thought the whole vicinage was haunted by her.* (*Silas Marner* by George Eliot)

victuals NOUN victuals means food ❑ *grumble a little over the victuals* (*The Adventures of Huckleberry Finn* by Mark Twain)

vintage NOUN vintage in this context means wine ❑ *Oh, for a draught of vintage!* (*Ode on a Nightingale* by John Keats)

virtual ADJ here virtual means powerful or strong ❑ *had virtual faith* (*The Prelude* by William Wordsworth)

vittles NOUN vittles is a slang word which means food ❑ *There never was such a woman for givin' away vittles and drink* (*Little Women* by Louisa May Alcott)

voided straight PHRASE voided straight is an old expression which means emptied immediately ❑ *see the rooms be voided straight* (*Doctor Faustus 4.1* by Christopher Marlowe)

wainscot NOUN wainscot is wood panel lining in a room so wainscoted means a room lined with wooden panels ❑ *in the dark wainscoted parlor* (*Silas Marner* by George Eliot)

walking the plank PHRASE walking the plank was a punishment in which a prisoner would be made to walk along a plank on the side of the ship and fall into the sea, where they would be abandoned ❑ *about hanging, and walking the plank* (*Treasure Island* by Robert Louis Stevenson)

want VERB want means to be lacking or short of ❑ *The next thing wanted was to get the picture framed* (*Emma* by Jane Austen)

wanting ADJ wanting means lacking or missing ❑ *wanting two fingers of the left hand* (*Treasure Island* by Robert Louis Stevenson)

wanting, I was not PHRASE I was not wanting means I did not fail ❑ *I was not wanting to lay a foundation of religious knowledge in his mind* (*Robinson Crusoe* by Daniel Defoe)

ward NOUN a ward is, usually, a child who has been put under the protection of the court or a guardian for his or her protection ❑ *I call the Wards in Jarndyce. They* *are caged up with all the others.* (*Bleak House* by Charles Dickens)

waylay VERB to waylay someone is to lie in wait for them or to intercept them ❑ *I must go up the road and waylay him* (*The Adventures of Huckleberry Finn* by Mark Twain)

weazen NOUN weazen is a slang word for throat. It actually means shrivelled ❑ *You with a uncle too! Why, I knowed you at Gargery's when you was so small a wolf that I could have took your weazen betwixt this finger and thumb and chucked you away dead* (*Great Expectations* by Charles Dickens)

wery ■ ADV very ❑ *Be wery careful o' vidders all your life* (*Pickwick Papers* by Charles Dickens) ■ *See* wibrated

wherry NOUN wherry is a small swift rowing boat for one person ❑ *It was flood tide when Daniel Quilp sat himself down in the wherry to cross to the opposite shore.* (*The Old Curiosity Shop* by Charles Dickens)

whether PREP whether means which of the two in this example ❑ *we came in full view of a great island or continent (for we knew not whether)* (*Gulliver's Travels* by Jonathan Swift)

whetstone NOUN a whetstone is a stone used to sharpen knives and other tools ❑ *I dropped pap's whetstone there too* (*The Adventures of Huckleberry Finn* by Mark Twain)

wibrated VERB in Dickens's use of the English language "w" often replaces "v" when he is reporting speech. So here "wibrated" means "vibrated". In *Pickwick Papers* a judge asks Sam Weller (who constantly confuses the two letters) "Do you spell it with a 'v' or a 'w'?" to which Weller replies "That depends upon the taste and fancy of the speller, my Lord" ❑ *There are strings . . . in the human heart that had better not be wibrated* (*Barnaby Rudge* by Charles Dickens)

wicket NOUN a wicket is a little door in a larger entrance ❑ *Having rested here, for a minute or so, to collect a good burst of sobs and an imposing show of tears and terror, he knocked loudly at the wicket* (*Oliver Twist* by Charles Dickens)

without CONJ without means unless ❑ *You don't know about me, without you have read a book by the name of The Adventures of Tom Sawyer* (*The Adventures of Huckleberry Finn* by Mark Twain)

wittles ■ NOUN wittles is a slang word which means food ❑ *I live on broken wittles–and I sleep on the coals* (*David Copperfield* by Charles Dickens) ■ *See* wibrated

woo VERB courts or forms a proper relationship with ❑ *before it woo* (*The Flea* by John Donne)

words, to have PHRASE if you have words with someone you have a disagreement or an argument ❑ *I do not want to have words with a young thing like you.* (*Black Beauty* by Anna Sewell)

workhouse NOUN workhouses were places where the homeless were given food and a place to live in return for doing very hard work ❑ *And the Union workhouses? demanded Scrooge. Are they still in operation?* (*A Christmas Carol* by Charles Dickens)

yawl NOUN a yawl is a small boat kept on a bigger boat for short trips. Yawl is also the name for a small fishing boat ❑ *She sent out her yawl, and we went aboard* (*The Adventures of Huckleberry Finn* by Mark Twain)

yeomanry NOUN the yeomanry was a collective term for the middle classes involved in agriculture ❑ *The yeomanry are precisely the order of people with whom I feel I can have nothing to do* (*Emma* by Jane Austen)

yonder ADV yonder means over there ❑ *all in the same second we seem to hear low voices in yonder!* (*The Adventures of Huckleberry Finn* by Mark Twain)